P9-EJH-797

STERN & WALZER

Three unknown Buddhist stories in an Arabic version

The MS of this book was completed in the summer of 1969 and handed over to the publishers shortly before S. M. Stern's untimely death in October 1969.

THREE UNKNOWN BUDDHIST STORIES

in an ARABIC VERSION

Introduction, Text & Translation

by

S. M. STERN & SOFIE WALZER

UNIVERSITY OF SOUTH CAROLINA PRESS
COLUMBIA, S.C. 29208

Published 1971 in Great Britain by
Bruno Cassirer (Publishers) Ltd., Oxford
and in the United States of America by
The University of South Carolina Press
Columbia, S.C.

International Standard Book Number: 0-87249-211-7

Library of Congress Catalog Card Number: 72-189034

Printed in Great Britain

Contents

Introduction

THE BOOK OF BALAWHAR AND BŪDĀSF

The transfer of the legend of the Buddha to the West is an arresting story. A form of the legend was translated into Persian—or, to be more accurate, into Middle Persian—perhaps by Manicheans attracted by the figure of the founder of a rival religion who exemplified their own ascetic tendencies. This version was rendered into Arabic by an unknown translator, presumably of the early Abbasid period (ca. A.D. 800) and in turn was translated—or rather paraphrased—into Georgian during the 9th century. Then the Christianization of the story began; it was completed in the Greek version, the legend of Barlaam and Joasaph, which was attributed to Saint John of Damascus (died about A.D. 750) and became a classic of Christian-Greek literature. Some modern scholars have argued that this attribution is wrong and that the book was translated into Greek from the Georgian version long after the time of the supposed author. However surprising this suggestion may sound, the arguments for it seem to be irrefutable, the most cogent being the fact that the Arabic version shows absolutely no trace of a Christian hand, while the Georgian represents the first stage of Christianization, which is fully carried through in the Greek text. The Greek text then becomes the source for the various Christian versions in East and West. In this way the Buddha and his instructor, Būdāsf and Balawhar, were transformed into Joasaph and Barlaam, apostles of Christianity in India.[1]

[1] On the Georgian version, and the relation of the Greek version to it, see the introduction by I. V. Abuladze to the English translation of the Georgian version by D. M. Lang, *The Balavariani*, London 1966. For the diffusion of the story see E. Kuhn, "Barlaam und Joasaph, eine bibliographisch-literargeschichtliche Studie", *Abhandlungen der k. bayer. Akademie der Wissenschaften*, xx (Munich 1893), and the extensive bibliography in H. Peri (Pflaum), *Der Religionsdisput der Barlaam-Legende, ein Motiv abendländischer Dichtung*, Salamanca 1959, pp. 223–62.

If this account of the derivation of the various versions is correct, the Arabic book of Balawhar and Būdāsf is the source of all the other versions; at any rate, since its Middle Persian original is lost, it is the most important witness for the early, non-Christianized, form of the story. The various forms of the Arabic text are known in outline, but have not been studied in detail. The present study is the first instalment of a series in which it is proposed to investigate the different Arabic texts and to make them more generally available.

The full text of the Arabic version has been published in a lithograph in Bombay in A.H. 1306/A.D. 1889. Until recently this lithograph was the only representative of the full text, since no MS of it was known either in India or anywhere else. This seemed somewhat strange, but the enigma can now be cleared up. The book was copied and read by the Ismā'īlīs of India, and it is to them that its preservation is due. A description of its contents is included in the 17th-century list of Ismā'īlī religious literature by Ismā'īl al-Majdū'. A MS copy came into the possession of the Library of the University of Bombay with the Fyzee collection, and thanks to the courtesy of the library authorities we possess photographs of it. Other copies are no doubt to be found in Ismā'īlī libraries in India, and the lithograph was also produced by Ismā'īlīs.[2]

Some time in the Middle Ages a summary was made of this long text—we may call it the "Bombay text"—of which two fragmentary MSS are known. One, a MS in Halle, was indeed the first text of the Arabic version to come to light, long before the Bombay lithograph made the full

---

[2] Ismā'īl al-Majdū', *Fahrasat al-Kutub wa'l-Rasā'il*, ed. 'Alī Naqī Munzawī, Teheran 1966, pp. 11–15; M. Goriawala, *A Descriptive Catalogue of the Fyzee Collection of Ismaili Manuscripts*, Bombay 1965, no. 169. The story is attributed by W. Ivanow (*A Guide to Ismaili Literature*, London 1933, no. 303 = *Ismaili Literature*, Teheran 1963, no. 314) to 'Abd al-Qādir Ḥakīm al-Dīn, who died in 1142/1730. This is obscure; does it refer to an individual elaboration of the theme, or to a redaction of the old text?

text available. Another MS of the epitome, preserved in Cairo, was identified by S. M. Stern.

Another important witness for the Arabic text is the long excerpt inserted by the tenth-century Shīʿite theologian Ibn Bābūya in one of his works. On the whole he also follows the Bombay text, though he abbreviates it considerably.[3]

THE THREE ADDITIONAL STORIES IN IBN BĀBŪYA'S EXCERPT

There is, however, in Ibn Bābūya's excerpt a long passage, containing three stories, which does not recur in the Bombay text—these are the stories edited in the present study. One hesitates to say whether this passage had originally formed part of the full text but was omitted in the Bombay text, or whether it was added to the original text in the version used by Ibn Bābūya. There are two, not quite conclusive, arguments in favour of the second alternative. First, as we shall see, one of the additional stories also circulated separately, so that it would be natural to assume that it was added by a reader who had a copy of it and added it—and the two other stories—to the original text in order to make the original more complete. This, however, could have been done by the original translator, or else the story could have been taken out of the book and circulated separately. The second argument is that the third story is in fact a second version of the legend of the Buddha's flight from his father's palace which is the subject-matter of the first half of the main story in which it is embedded; the possibility, however, cannot be entirely excluded that the original author of the Arabic version was responsible for this clumsy joining of two doubles of the same story. Though there is no certainty, one is nevertheless inclined to assume that the three stories did not belong to the original Arabic version, but were added afterwards.

[3] A short sketch of the Arabic tradition was given by S. M. Stern in the *Bulletin of the School of Oriental and African Studies*, 1959, pp. 150–1. (It was there stated that no manuscripts of the complete—"Bombay"—version were known. This is no longer true, since manuscripts of this version are preserved by the Ismāʿīlīs of India.)

THE STORY OF THE KING'S GREY HAIR

The first story is about a king who arranges a great military review in order to enjoy the show of his might. Having looked at the splendour of his realm, he wants to inspect his own face in a mirror, but discovers a grey hair, a messenger of death against which his courtiers profess to be powerless. The realization that death is inevitable brings about the king's conversion. The story is clearly a variant of the stories about the *devadutta*, the "messengers of death", the classic representative of which is the *Makhadeva Jātaka*. This is about Makhadeva, king of Mithila, who asks his barber to see whether he can find a grey hair in his beard. The barber does find a grey hair, which is taken by the king as a sign of approaching death:

> Lo these grey hairs that on my head appear
> Are death's own messengers that come to rob
> My life. 'Tis time I turned from wordly things
> And in the hermit's path sought saving peace.[4]

A closely related version is part of the *Nimi Jātaka*. A king told his barber to inform him when he finds a grey hair. When the barber so reports, the king renounces the world and makes his son his successor, reciting:

> Lo these grey hairs that on my head appear
> Take of my life in passing year by year.
> They are God's messengers, which bring to mind
> The time I must renounce the world is near.

A similar story about the barber forms the beginning of the *Culla-Sutasoma Jātaka*.[5]

---

[4] *The Jātaka*, C.U.P. 1895–1913, vol. i 30 ff.; T. W. Rhys Davids, *Buddhist Birth Stories*, pp. 186 ff.; D. Andersen, *Pali Reader*, p. 121.

[5] *The Nimi Jātaka*, ibid. vol. vi, 53–4; *Culla-Sutasoma Jātaka*, ibid. vol. v, 92; cf. also vol. iii, 238.

In other stories there is a question of three messengers of death encountered by the hero: an old man, a sick man, and a corpse.[6]

The idea that grey hairs are the first signs of approaching decay is of course obvious[7]—yet there can be no doubt that our story is the faithful translation of some Buddhist original. Not only is the expression "messenger of death" (*rasūl al-mawt*) the exact equivalent of the term *devadutta*, but the whole *mise en scène*, with the elaborate (and largely irrelevant) account of the king's antecedents, the long discussions, the careful painting of the background of the main event, bear witness to the origin of the piece. In his paragraph on "Books by the Persians, Greeks, Indians and Arabs containing admonitions, maxims and wise sayings, either by known or unknown authors" the 10th-century bibliographer Ibn al-Nadīm mentions the following title: "The book about the king with the grey hair, and the dispute which he had with his counsellors and the people of his kingdom".[8] It is beyond reasonable doubt that this title refers to our story, the main points of which are exactly the king's discovery of his grey hair and the subsequent conversations in which he upbraids his counsellors for their helplessness. Though the paragraph contains titles of Arabic originals as well as of translations, in this part of the paragraph the titles are those of books of foreign provenance, so that Ibn al-Nadīm knew that the story, which he had probably seen in an independent form, was a translation. We have already discussed the implications of the story

[6] See R. Morris, "Devaduta, Death Messengers. An old story with modern variations", *Journal of the Pali Text Society*, 1885, pp. 62 ff. A version of the story is included in Grimm's Fairy-tales ("Die Boten des Todes", larger ed., vol. vii, no. 177); in Bolte's and Polivka's commentary on the Fairy-tales there is a rich collection of references to versions in many languages.

[7] Cf. *Anwār-i Suhaylī*, transl. Eastwick, p. 72: "The white hair comes, its message gives from fate and terror's kind, And the crooked back and stooping form Death's salutation". This happens to be at hand; no doubt many similar passages could be found.

[8] Ibn al-Nadīm, *al-Fihrist*, p. 316.

appearing here independently and said that it cannot be decided with certainty whether originally it was translated as an isolated story or was detached from some collection—possibly from the book of Balawhar and Būdāsf; though it would be more natural to assume that it was inserted in that book by a later reader. At any rate, though no Indian original seems to be known of this version of the story of the grey hair of the king, we may be fairly certain that it did exist, so that the Arabic version restores to us a lost Buddhist story.

THE STORY OF THE SKULL—IS IT A KING'S OR A PAUPER'S?

There was a king, who, after a good beginning, became evil. He has a trusted counsellor who wishes to reform him, and for this purpose repeatedly stamps with his foot upon a human skull in the king's presence. Finally the king asks him about the meaning of his action, upon which he explains that he had found the skull near the royal tombs, and took it home in order to wrap it up in precious brocade—hoping that in this way he would confirm whether the skull was really that of a king, since if it was, the honour shown to it would restore it to its pristine beauty. But neither honour nor abuse made any difference to it. Thus it remained uncertain whether the skull belonged to a king or to a pauper, and the sages were no more able to enlighten him. He brought it along in order that the king should help him in his perplexity: if it is the skull of a pauper, why was it found in the royal tombs? If it is the skull of a king what a lesson of the transience of royal glory! The king took the admonishment to heart.

No Buddhist or other Indian parallel is known to us. The notion that in death king and pauper are alike is universal; "the small and great are there", says the Book of Job (iii, 19), and no doubt many such passages could be quoted from many places and many times. A saying quoted from a Greek sage in Ḥunayn b. Isḥāq's collection of apophthegms (mid-9th century) is more to the point: "I wanted to distinguish the bones of their slaves from the bones of their kings, but found them equal".[9] The characteristic *mise en scène* again suggests that we have here the translation of an unknown Indian story expressing this general truth.

We have on purpose left out an additional motive in the story. When the king takes no notice of his misbehaviour in trampling the skull, the counsellor re-appears, and in addition to the skull, carries a balance, weighs out a dram of dust, and puts the dust into the eyeholes and the mouth of the skull. As an explanation he offers the reflection that the eye, which could not be filled with all that is under the heaven, and the mouth, which nothing could satiate, could now be filled with a little dust.

The earliest form of the story is found in the Babylonian Talmud (*Tāmīd*, 32b): When Alexander reaches the gate of Paradise, he is given a ball. "He went and weighed all his silver and gold against it, and it was not equal to it. He said to the Rabbis: 'How is this?' They replied: 'It is the eyeball of a human being, which is never satisfied.' He said to them: 'How can you prove that it is so?' They took a little dust and covered it, and immediately it was weighed down; and so it is written: The nether world and destruction are never satisfied; so the eyes of man are never satisfied [Proverbs, xxvii, 20]".[10] The moral, though this is not made explicit, applies particularly to Alexander, the very exemplar of an insatiable world-conqueror. This is brought out clearly in the early Arabic form of the story,

---

[9] *Nawādir al-Falāsifa*, MS Munich 651, fol. 79r: *aradtu an umayyiza 'iẓāma 'abīdihim min 'iẓāmi mulūkihim fa-wajadtuhā sawā'a.*; in Judah al-Ḥarīzī's Hebrew translation, ed. Loewenthal, ii, 5, 21 (p. 31). Cf. Moses b. Ezra's Hebrew poem (Spain, 11th-12th century): "When I looked at them, I could not distinguish between slaves and masters" (no. 152, line 3; cf. no. 51, line 3, and no. 177, line 3).

[10] The translation is by M. Simon, in the Soncino Press translation of the Talmud.

included by Ibn Hishām (d. 829 or 834) in his *Book of Crowns* on the authority of the story-teller Wahb b. Munabbih (d. 728 or 729).[11] Dhu'l-Qarnayn receives a stone from the guardian of the white house in the Land of the Angels. The prophet al-Khaḍir explains this as an allusion to his eyes: "the whole contents of the world cannot fill your eyes . . . but *this* will fill them"—and takes a handful of dust and puts it into one of the scales of a balance, the stone into the other; the dust weighs down the stone. (It does not matter at all that according to Ibn Hishām Dhu'l-Qarnayn is not identical with Alexander, but is one of the legendary South Arabian kings whose "history" he purported to write in that book; this story certainly comes from the cycle of Alexander, to whom the name Dhu'l-Qarnayn is generally applied, and was artificially transferred into the South Arabian saga.)

The story seems to have been invented as an illustration for an old proverb: "Man's eye is not satisfied till it is filled with dust." A somewhat more elaborate version of the proverb is found in a late version of the ancient story of Aḥīqar ("Man's eye is like a fountain and is not satisfied with possessions until it is filled with earth")—it is likely that this, or a simpler form, already figured in older versions. We have already encountered Proverbs, xxvii, 20, very properly recalled in the Talmud in connection with the story of Alexander and the eyeball. The proverb remained current until modern times in Islamic countries.[12] A secondary form ("Nothing can fill man's *belly* except dust") was even considered as part of a divine revelation originally belonging to the Koran, and was adopted in a later Muslim

---

[11] The passage was published by M. Lidzbarski in *Zeitschrift für Assyriologie*, viii (1893), 304; it is included in the edition of the full text, Hyderabad 1347, p. 102. For the different versions of the story see R. Hartmann, "Alexander und der Rätselstein aus dem Paradies", *A Volume of Oriental Studies presented to E. G. Browne*, Cambridge 1922, pp. 179 ff.

[12] For the Aḥīqar story cf. Th. Nöldeke, *Untersuchungen zum Achiqar-Roman*, and Hartmann, p. 181; for the proverbs Nöldeke p. 44, and Hartmann, p. 182.

version of the Alexander novel.[13] Apart from the story under discussion, the anecdote about the eyeball which is only outweighed by dust—which can be considered as an elaboration of the proverb—is always connected with Alexander; but it is not, of course, impossible that it also circulated in other forms. It seems obvious that its insertion into the story about the impossibility of distinguishing between the skull of a king and a pauper is secondary. The two stories have quite different morals; the one intends to illustrate the equality in death of king and pauper, the other the end in death of all human appetite. It is impossible to say at which stage the story about the eyeball was introduced into the story about the skull—whether in India, in Persia, or only by a Muslim redactor; or to know whether the man who introduced the story about the eyeball heard it as an anecdote connected with Alexander or as an anonymous anecdote.

THE STORY OF THE PRINCE WHO REALIZING THE TRANSITORINESS OF THE WORLD FLED FROM HIS PALACE AND HIS WIFE, AND REFUSED TO RETURN TO THE STATE FROM WHICH HE HAD JUST ESCAPED

The story is composed of two parts, the first of which leads up to the climax, the prince's flight from his palace and his wife. This story is in fact merely a version of the story of the Buddha's four encounters, with some particular features. At the very beginning, the story tells how when the prince was still an infant, he made three steps, uttering words which indicated the three stages of human destiny:

[13] Nöldeke-Schwally, *Geschichte des Qorans*, i, 234 ff., Hartmann, p. 181. (Hartmann writes: "I see no decisive argument against attributing this saying . . . to Muḥammad. But it is obviously a proverb taken up by Muḥammad". Quite so—but there is of course no more reason *for* attributing the saying to Muḥammad than a thousand other sayings ascribed to him.)

You will be agile, then you will become old, and then you will die. According to Buddhist legends the new-born Buddha made seven steps and uttered some words—though of a different character.[14] There follows the account of the prince's encounters with a sick man then with an old man and finally with a corpse—closely following the story of the Buddha. There is, however, a fourth "encounter" of which we find no parallel: the prince, asking about an old rafter supporting the roof, learns that it had once been a living tree. The scene of the prince's separation from his wife again conforms with the story of the Buddha, but the colourful scene is here merely sketched.

The second part of the story tells of the prince's flight from his father's city, with a companion whom he met in the street, and of how the princess of the city where he arrives in the guise of a poor wanderer sees him from the window, falls in love with him and wants to marry him. The prince tells four stories in which men have horrifying experiences with women; when all is over, the moral is drawn—would they be prepared to undergo the same experience again? This part is at variance with the stories of the Buddha's flight from his palace.[15] It probably belongs to a quite different story about a prince who leaves his wife and refuses to marry again; its first part was then interpolated with incidents from the legend of the Buddha.

Of the four examples framed into this story, the first, about the prince who in his drunkenness mistook a corpse

---

[14] The canonical account is given in the "Discourse of the Wondrous and Marvellous Events" in which the favourite disciple Ānanda recites to the Buddha the events of the conception and the birth. "As soon as born the Bodhisatta firmly standing with even feet goes towards the north with seven long steps, a white parasol being held over him [by the gods]. He surveys all the quarters and in a lordly voice says, 'I am the chief in the world, I am the best in the world, I am the first in the world. This is my last birth. There is now no existence again". The same story occurs in the continuous accounts given in the *Nidānakathā* and the *Lalita-Vistara*. See E. J. Thomas, *The Life of Buddha as Legend and History*, London 1927, pp. 29, 33.

[15] Thomas, pp. 54 ff.

for his wife, is not found in Indian literature. A Turkish version, made by the Manicheans of Central Asia, has, however, been found among the manuscripts discovered in Turfan.[16] Since a single leaf only has been found, it is impossible to say what the book containing the story was: a Turkish version of the same frame-story which we have in Arabic, or some other collection of stories. The second example is the rather inept story about thieves who stole a chest which they thought was full of gold, but which instead contained snakes; no Indian model is known to us. Nor is one for the story of the prince and his liberation from prison. On the other hand, the story of the she-demon who devoured shipwrecked sailors as has been already pointed out by Oldenburg and Kuhn, has many Buddhist parallels.[17] The *ghūl*, "she demon", is the translation of *rākshasī*.

THE ARABIC STYLE OF THE STORIES

One is struck by the awkward Arabic style; there are phrases so strange that some concentration is needed before the meaning can be grasped. It is a far cry indeed from the fluent Arabic of Ibn al-Muqaffa''s version of the *Kalīla wa-Dimna* which rightly became a classic of Arabic style. The whole of the book of Balawhar and Būdāsf shows a similarly heavy style. This need not necessarily mean that our stories did after all belong to the book from the very beginning, since the similarity may be explained by the texts having been produced by the same school of translators. A detailed stylistic examination is needed before more definite conclusions can be drawn.

---

[16] A. v. Le Coq, *Türkische Manichaica aus Chotschöi'* (Abhandlungen der preussischen Akademie der Wissenschaften, 1911, pp. 5–7; S. von Oldenburg, in the *Bulletin de l'Académie Imperiale de St.-Pétersbourg*, 1912, pp. 779–82; W. Bang, in *Le Muséon*, 1931, p. 12.

[17] Kuhn, p. 81, Cf. also D. Andersen, *Pali Reader*, p. 119 (we owe this reference to Sir Harold Bailey). The chief texts are the Jātaka no. 196 (translated in *The Jatakas*, ii, 89).

The stories are told to the prince Būdāsf by the wise Balawhar in order to illustrate his teaching about repentance being always acceptable to God.

THE TEXT

Since we are editing some pages from Ibn Bābūya's book, ideally we should have examined all the manuscripts of the book and established our text according to the results. This we could not do, but think that for all practical purposes the material of which we have availed ourselves is sufficient. As far as we could see, there are no old MSS of the book, so that, there being no MS which would on the face of it promise a superior text, we have chosen the most easily accessible MSS. These were the MSS preserved in the Berlin and Manchester collections.

> Manchester, John Rylands Library 802, copied by Muḥammad b. Ḥājjī, in Ramaḍāir 1041/1631.
> Berlin 2721, copied in Isfahan by ʿAbd Allāh b. ʿAlī al-Riḍā al-Khādim al-Nakhafī, in Rajab 1082/1671.

In addition we have used the Teheran lithograph dated 1301/18, 83–4 in which the text occurs on pp. 345–56.

These three direct witnesses were not, however, our only resource. The story of Balawhar and Būdāsf was reproduced from Ibn Bābūya's book in the *Biḥār al-Anwār*, the great encyclopaedia of Shīʿite lore compiled at the end of the 17th century by Majlisī. The story is found on pp. 220 ff. of vol. xvii of the Teheran lithograph, the portion edited here on pp. 236 ff. Majlisī's text represents of course the MS used by him.

Majlisī also translated the story of *Balawhar wa-Būdāsf* into Persian in order to include it in his Persian ethical book called *ʿAyn al-Ḥayāt* (pp. 315–87 in the Teheran edition 1372/1952–3). The Persian text of the story in the British Museum Or. 3529 is merely an extract from the *ʿAyn al-Ḥayāt*, made by an 18th-century scribe. Another extract figures in

Muḥammad Muḥsin's historical compilation, *Zubdat al-Tawārīkh*, dated 1154/18.[18]

It so happened that this late offspring of Ibn Bābūya's version was the first to have come to the attention of modern scholarship. The British Museum MS drew the attention of the Sanskrit scholar S. von Oldenburg and was first briefly described by V. von Rosen in a note entitled "A Persian recension of the story of Barlam and Joasaph", and published in the *Papers of the Oriental Department of the Imperial Russian Archaeological Commission*, in 1882,[19] whereas next year (pp. iv, 229–65) Oldenburg himself gave a detailed account in the same periodical and under the same title as that of Rosen's article. Since the British Museum text contained the information that the story goes back to Ibn Bābūya, Rosen and Hommel (who has great merits for the study of the Arabic versions of the story) identified the extract in Ibn Bābūya's *Kamāl al-Dīn wa-Tamām al-Niʿma*, of which they used the Berlin MS.[20] In 1895, when describing the British Museum MS, Rieu was led by the heading of the extract in the *Zubdat al-Tawārīkh*, which gives as its source the *ʿAyn al-Ḥayāt* of Āqā Muḥammad Bāqir (Majlisī) to conclude that it was perhaps Majlisī who translated into Persian the Arabic text of Ibn Bābūya. That the Persian translation indeed comes from the *ʿAyn al-Hayāt* has now been verified, and that it was Majlisī himself who made the translation, is very likely, especially since he has included the Arabic text in his *Biḥār al-Anwār*. The existence of this quotation in the *Biḥār* has hitherto remained unknown. Now the circle is closed: the original Arabic text of Ibn Bābūya's version was included by Majlisī in his *Biḥār al-Anwār*, and a Persian translation (probably made by himself) in his *ʿAyn al-Ḥayāt*. The excerpts

---

[18] Ch. Rieu. *Supplement to the Catalogue of the Persian Manuscripts in the British Museum*, London 1895, no. 380.

[19] *Zapiski Vostochnavo Otdeleniya Imperatorskavo Russkavo Arkheologicheskavo Obshchestva*, vol. iii, pp. 273–6.

[20] Rosen, "Again on Ibn Bābawayh and Barlaam", ibid., iv, 397–400. Cf. Kuhn, p. 14.

in the British Museum MS and in the *Zubdat al-Tawārīkh* were then derived from the *'Ayn al-Ḥayāt*. The Persian versions may be of some interest as recent branches of the tradition of the *Balawhar wa-Būdāsf* story, and the British Museum MS rendered the service of first acquainting modern scholars with Ibn Bābūya's version, the only one to contain the stories published here; but now they can add nothing to the establishment of the text, for which we can use directly their model, the Arabic text available to Majlisī, which he inserted in the *Biḥār*.

TEXT

AND

TRANSLATION

I

زعموا أنه كان فى زمن ملك عظيم الصوت فى العلم ، رفيق ،
سائس ، يحب العدل فى أمته ، والإصلاح لرعيّته . عاش
بذلك زمانا بخير حال . ثم هلك فجزعت عليه أمته . وكان
بامرأة له حمل ؛ فذكر المنجمون والكهنة أنه غلام . وكان
يدبّر مُلكهم مَن كان يلى ذلك فى زمان مَلكهم . فاتفق 5
الأمر كما ذكره المنجمون والكهنة ، ووُلد من ذلك الحمل غلام .
فأقاموا عند ميلاده سنة بالمعازف والملاهى والأشربة والأطعمة .
ثم إن أهل العلم منهم والفقه والربّانيين قالوا لعامّتهم :
إنْ كان هذا المولود إنّما هو هبة من الله تعالى فقد جعلتم
الشكر لغيره ، وإنْ كان هبة من غير الله عزّ وجلّ فقد 10
أدّيتم الحق إلى مَن أعطاكموه ، واجتهدتم فى الشكر لمَن
رزقكموه . فقالت لهم العامّة : ما وهبه لنا إلا الله تبارك
وتعالى ، ولا امتنّ به علينا غيره . قالت العلماء : فإنْ كان
الله عزّ وجلّ هو الذى وهبه لكم فقد أرضيتم غير الذى
أعطاكم ، وأسخطتم الله الذى وهبه لكم . فقالت لهم الرعيّة : 15
فأشيروا علينا أيّها الحكماء ، وأخبرونا أيّها العُلماء ؛
فنتبع قولكم ، ونقبل نصيحتكم ، ومُرونا بأمركم .
قالت العلماء : فإنّا نرى لكم أنْ تعدلوا عن اتباع مَرضاة
الشيطان بالمعازف والملاهى والمسكر ، إلى ابتغاء مَرضاة الله
عزّ وجلّ ، وشكره على ما أنعم به عليكم أضعاف شكركم 20
للشيطان ؛ حتى يغفرَ لكم ما كان منكم . قالت الرعيّة :
لا تحمل أجسادنا كلّ الذى قلتم وأمرتم به . قالت العلماء :
يا أولى الجهل ! كيف أطعتم مَن لا حقّ له عليكم ، وتعصون مَن له

A = Berlin MS; B = Manchester MS; L = lithographed edition; M = Majlisī.

8 العلم: A adds والمعرفة || 9 كان om AM || 9 تعالى AM عزوجل BL || 9 فقد: AB وقد LM || 11 أعطاكموه AM أعطاكم BL 12 فقالت L وقالت B فقال AM || 13 العلماء ABM الحكماء L || 13 قالت L قال ABM || 14 أرضيتم AM رضيتم, L راضيتم B || 16 وأخبرونا AM وبصّرونا BL || 18 قالت LM قال A om. B || 19 والمسكر AM والشكر BL

THE STORY OF THE KING'S GREY HAIR

It is reported that once upon a time there was a king, very renowned for his knowledge, gentle, a good ruler who liked justice to prevail amongst his people and prosperity to spread to his subjects; he lived in that way happily for a time. Then he passed away and his people mourned him. Now one of his wives was with child. The astrologers and soothsayers said that it would be a boy. The same man administered the kingdom who used to do it at the time of the former king. Then it happened as the astrologers and soothsayers had said, and that wife bore a boy. To celebrate his birth, they passed a year in music and merrymaking and drinking and eating.

Then the sages and law scholars and theologians among them said to the common people: "If this child is a gift of God, you have given thanks to somebody else; but if he is a gift from somebody other than God, then you have paid your due to him who has given it to you and shown yourself zealous in thanking him who bestowed him on you." The common people replied: "Nobody else but God has given him to us and nobody else granted him to us". Said the sages: "But if it was God Who gave him to you, you have pleased somebody else who did not give him to you and angered God Who gave him to you." The subjects replied to them: "Advise us then, oh you wise men, and inform us, oh you sages, and we shall follow your words and will accept your council. Order us what to do". Said the sages: "We think you ought to give up complying with the wish of Satan in merrymaking and music and drinking and turn to complying with the wish of God and to thank Him twice as much for what He has bestowed on you than you thanked Satan, so that He may pardon you for what you have done." Said the subjects: "Our bodies cannot bear all that you say and command." Said the sages: "Oh you ignorant people how could you have obeyed Satan

الحق الواجب عليكم ؟ وكيف قويتم على مالا ينبغى، وتضعفون
عمّا ينبغى ؟ قالوا لهم : يا أئمّة الحكماء ! عظُمت فينا الشهوات
وكثرت فينا اللذّات ، فقوينا بما عظُم فينا منها على العظيم
من شكلها ، وضعُفت منّا النيّات ، فعجزنا عن حمل
المثقلات . فارضوا منّا فى الرجوع عن ذلك يومًا فيومًا ، 5
ولا تكلّفونا كلّ هذا الثقل . قالوا لهم : يامعشر السفهاء!
ألستم أبناء الجهل ، وإخوان الضّلال ، حين خفّت عليكم
الشقوة ، وثقلت عليكم السعادة ؟! قالوا لهم : أيّها
السادة الحكماء ، والقادة العلماء ! إنّا نستجير من
تعنيفكم إيّانا بمغفرة الله عزّ وجلّ ، ونستتر من تعييركم 10
لنا بعفوه . ولا توبّخونا ، ولا تعيّرونا بضعفنا ، ولا تعيبوا
الجهالة علينا ؛ فإنّا إنْ أطعنا الله ، مع عفوه وحلمه
وتضعيفه الحسنات ، واجتهدنا فى عبادته مثل الذى
بذلنا لِهَوانا من الباطل - بلغْنا حاجتنا ، وبلغ الله عزّ
وجلّ بنا غايتنا ، ورحمنا كما خلقنا . فلمّا قالوا ذلك أقرّ 15
لهم علماؤهم ، ورضوا قولهم . فصلّوا وصاموا وتعبّدوا
وعظّموا الصدقات سنة كاملة .

فلمّا انقضى ذلك منهم قالت الكهنة : إنّ الذى صنعت هذه الأمّة
على هذا المولود يخبر أنّ هذا المَلِك يكون فاجرا ويكون بارّا بهم ،
ويكون متجبّرا ويكون متواضعا ، ويكون مسيئا ويكون محسنا. 20
وقال المنجّمون مثل ذلك . فقيل لهم : كيف قلتم ذلك ؟ قالت الكهنة:
قلنا هذا من قِبَل اللهو والمعازف والباطل الذى صُنع عليه ، وماصُنع
عليه من ضدّه بعد ذلك . وقال المنجّمون : قلنا ذلك من قِبَل
استقامة الزهرة والمشترى .

---

[11] ولا توبّخونا L فلا تؤنّبونا M ولا تنوبون A ,, [17] وعظّموا AM وأعظموا L || [18] قالت LM. قال AB [19] بهم om AM

who has no real claim over you and resist now Him Who has a compelling claim on you? How could you be strong enough to do what ought not be done and how are you now too weak to do what ought to be done?" They replied: "Oh you mighty sages, the desires were strong in us and numerous the pleasures, and through their strength we were able to go to excesses which match them, for our good intentions are weak and therefore we cannot support heavy burdens. Be satisfied then if we withdraw from that day by day, and do not impose on us all this burden." They said to them: "Oh you stupid crowd, are you not sons of ignorance and brethren of error since wretchedness sits lightly upon you and felicity is too heavy for you?" They answered them: "Oh you wise masters and wise leaders: We seek protection from your rebuke in the forgiveness of God the Almighty and we hide from your reproach in His pardon. Do not reprimand us and do not reproach us for our weakness and do not blame us for ignorance; for if we obey God, Who is forgiving and long-suffering and repays good actions doubly, and we make an effort to serve Him as we had hitherto pandered to our vain desires, then we obtain what we want, God will make us reach our aims and will take pity on us as He has created us." When they had said that, the sages were pleased with them and they agreed with their words. So they prayed and fasted and worshipped and gave alms plentifully a whole year.

When this period had elapsed the soothsayers said: "What these people have done for this child indicates that this king will be partly bad and will be partly good and he will be partly haughty and he will be partly humble and he will do evil and he will do good things." The astrologers said the same things. And it was said to them: "How are you able to say this?" So the soothsayers said: "We have said that because of the merrymaking and the music and all the futile things which were done on his behalf and because of the opposite things which were done on his behalf afterwards". And the astrologers answered: "We have said that because Venus and Saturn were in power at the time of his birth."

فنشأ الغلام بكبر لا يوصف عظمة، ومرح لا ينعت، وعدوان لا يطاق. فعسف وجار وظلم فى الحكم وغشم. وكان أحبّ النّاس إليه مَن وافقه على ذلك، وأبغض النّاس إليه مَن خالفه فى شىء من ذلك. واغترّ بالشباب والصحّة والقدرة والظفر والنصر؛ فامتلأ سرورا وإعجابا بما هو فيه، ورآى كلّ ما يحبّه، وسمع كلّ ما اشتهى؛ حتى بلغ اثنتين وثلاثين سنة.

ثم جمع نساء من بنات المُلوك وصبيانا وجواريه المخدّرات وخيْله المطهمات العتاق، وألوان مراكبه الفاخرة ووصائفه وخدّامه الذين يكون خدمته. فأمرهم أن يلبسوا أجدّ ثيابهم ويتزيّنوا بأحسن زينتهم. وأمر ببناء مجلس مقابل مطلع الشمس، صفائح أرضه الذهب، مفصّصًا بألوان الجواهر، طوله مائة وعشرون ذراعا، وعرضه ستّون ذراعا، مزخرفا سقفه وحيطانه، قد زُيّن بكرائم الحلىّ، وصنوف النظم وفاخره. وأمر بضروب الأموال فأخرجت من الخزائن، ونضّدت سماطين أمام مجلسه. وأمر جنوده وأصحابه وقوّاده وكتّابه وحجّابه وعظماء أهل بلاده وعلماءهم؛ فحضروا فى أحسن هيئتهم وأجمل جمالهم، وتسلّح فرسانه وركبت خيوله فى عدّتهم؛ ثم وقفوا على مراكزهم ومراتبهم صفوفا وكراديس. وإنّما أراد بزعمه أن ينظر إلى منظر رفيع حسن يسرّبه نفسه، ويقرّبه عينه. ثم خرج فصعد إلى مجلسه، وأشرف على مملكته؛ فخرّوا له سُجّدا.

فقال لبعض علمائه: قد نظرت من مملكتى

---

6 يحبّه AM يحبّ BL || 9 المطهمات AM المطهمة BL || 23 غلمانه BM

So the boy grew up with great arrogance the strength of which passes description, and in equally indescribable high spirits and with aggressiveness which was unbearable; and he was oppressive, unjust and tyrannical in his judgment, and rude, and he was most fond of the people who agreed with him about what he was doing and he disliked the people who contradicted him in anything of that. He was misled by his youth and his health and by power and triumph and victory, and he was filled with joy and self-satisfaction and he saw all that he liked and he heard all that he wished until he reached the age of thirty-two years.

Then he assembled his wives, who were daughters of kings, and young men, and his slave girls from the harem, and his horses, perfectly beautiful and of noble race, and luxurious riding beasts, and servants and attendants who were in his service. And he ordered them to put on their newest dresses and to embellish themselves with their best ornaments. Then he gave orders for the building of a hall facing the rising of the sun. The plates of its floor were made from gold incrusted with various kinds of jewels; its length was 120 cubits, and its width 60 cubits.

Its ceiling and its walls were decorated with pieces of precious stone and all kinds of precious pearls. He gave orders for all sorts of treasures and they were brought out from his stores and were spread out in two rows in front of the hall. Then he gave orders to his army and his companions and his officers and his scribes and the chamberlains and the grandees and scholars of the people of his country. They all appeared in their best attire and as beautiful as they possibly could be. His knights put on their weapons and his cavalry rode about in their full attire; then they established themselves in their positions and ranks in rows and cohorts. His intention in all this was to look on a grand and beautiful spectacle which could give him joy and satisfaction. Then he went out and went up to the hall and looked at his kingdom, and the people prostrated themselves before him.

إلى منظر حسن ، وبقى أن أنظر إلى صورة وجهى . فدعا
بمرآة فنظر إلى وجهه ؛ فبينا هو يقلّب طرفه فيها إذْ
لاحت له شعرة بيضاء من لحيته كغراب أبيض بين
غربان سُود . فاشتدّ منها ذعره وفزعه ، وتغيّر فى
5 عينه حاله ، وظهرت الكآبة والحزن فى وجهه ، وتولّى
السرور عنه . ثم قال فى نفسه : هذا حين نعى إلىّ
شبابى ، وبيّن لى أنّ مُلكى فى ذهاب ، وأوذنت بالنزول
عن سرير مُلكى . ثم قال : هذه مقدّمة الموت ورسول
البلى ، لم يحجبه عنى حاجب ، ولم يمنعه عنى حارس ؛
10 فنعى إلىّ نفسى ، وآذننى بزوال مُلكى . ما أسرع هذا فى
تبديل بهجتى ، وذهاب سرورى ، وهدْم قوّتى ! ولم تمنعه
منى الحصون ، ولم تدفعه عنى الجنود . هذا سالب الشباب
والقوّة ، وماحق العزّ والثروة ، ومفرّق الشمل ، وقاسم
التراث بين الأولياء والأعداء ؛ مفسد المعاش ، ومنغّص
15 اللذّات ، ومخرّب العمارات ، ومشتّت الجمع ، وواضع
الرفيع ، ومذلّ المنيع ؛ قد أناخت بى أثقاله ، ونصب لى حباله .
ثم نزل عن مجلسه حافيا ماشيا ، وقد صعد إليه محمولا .

ثم جمع إليه جنوده ، ودعا إليه ثقاته فقال : أيّها الملأ !
ماذا صنعت بكم ؟ وما آتيت إليكم منذ ملكتكم ووليّت أموركم ؟
20 قالوا له : أيّها الملك المحمود ! عظم بلاؤك عندنا ، وهذه
أنفسنا مبذولة فى طاعتك ؛ فمرْنا بأمرك . قال : طرقنى
عدوّ مخيف ؛ لم تمنعونى منه حتى نزل بى وكنتم عدّتى وثقاتى.

---

5 عينه AM عينيه BL || 7 فى AM إلى BL || 10 وآذننى M وآذنى A وآذن لى L
|| 19 ملكتكم: وليتكم A || 20 له om AB || 19 بكم AL فيكم BM || بى B
21 قال LM فقال AB

Then he said to one of his pages: "Now I have looked at the beauty of my kingdom, it is left to me now to look at the shape of my face." And he called for a mirror and looked at his face and while he let his look roam about on it, behold, there appeared a white hair in his beard like a white raven amongst black ravens; and his terror and fright because of this was great and in his eyes his whole condition was changed and grief and sorrow appeared on his face and joy turned away from him. Then he said to himself: "This is the time when the death of my youth is announced to me and when it is explained to me that my kingdom is about to disappear and I am warned to descend from the throne of my kingdom." Then he said: "This is the vanguard of death and the messenger of decay from whom no chamberlain has shielded me and whom no watchman has kept away from me, and it announces to me the death of myself and tells me about the loss of my kingdom; how quickly this was able to change my delight and make my joy disappear and to destroy my strength. No fortresses kept it away from me and no army warded it off me. It is the one that snatches away my youth and my strength and that does away with my glory and wealth and the one that separates what is united, and distributes the inheritance amongst friends and foes, that destroys life, spoils pleasures and demolishes buildings, that separates the company and humbles that which is high and makes low that which is mighty; its weight has pulled me down and laid a snare for me." Then he came down from his seat in the hall walking barefoot whilst he had been carried up to it.

Then he gathered his army and he called his intimates to his presence and said: "Oh elders! What is it that I have done to you and what have I given to you since the time that I became your King and ruled over you?" They answered him: "Oh praiseworthy king, you have deserved very well of us and we are willing to spend our lives in obedience to you; so give us your orders." He said: "A fearful enemy has knocked at my door whom you did not ward off from me, so that he has decended upon me, although

قالوا : أيّها الملك ! أين هذا العدوّ ؟ أيُرى أم لا يُرى؟
قال : يُرى أثره ، ولا يُرى عينه . قالوا : أيّها الملك !
هذه عدّتنا كما ترى ، وعندنا سكن ، وفينا ذوو الحجى
والنُّهى ؛ فأرِناه نكْفِكَ ما مثله يُكفى . قال : قد عظم
الاغترار منى بكم ، ووضعتُ الثقة فى غير موضعها ؛
حين اتخذتكم وجعلتكم لنفسى جُنّة ، وإنّما بذلتُ
لكم الأموال ورفعت شرفكم وجعلتكم البطانة دون
غيركم لتحفظونى من الأعداء وتحرسونى منهم ؛ ثم أيّدتكم
على ذلك بتشييد البلدان وتحصين المدائن والثقة من السلاح،
ونحّيتُ عنكم الهموم ، وفرّغتكم للنجدة والاحتفاظ، ولم أكن
أخشى أن أُراع معكم ، ولا أتخوّف المنون على بنيانى وأنتم عكوف
مطيفون به ؛ فطُرقت وأنتم حولى ، وأُتيتُ وأنتم معى ؛ فلئن كان هذا
ضعفا منكم فما أخذت أمرى بثقة ، وإن كانت غفلة منكم فما
أنتم بأهل النصيحة ، ولا علىّ بأهل الشفقة .

قالوا : أيّها الملك ! أمّا شىء نطيق دفعه بالخيل والقوّة فليس
بواصل إليك إن شاء الله ونحن أحياء ، وأمّا ما لا يُرى فقد غُيِّبَ
عنّا علمه ، وعجزت قوّتنا عنه . قال : أليس اتخذتكم لتمنعونى من
عدوّى ؟ قالوا : بلى . قال : فمن أىّ عدوّ تحفظونى ؟ من الذى
يضرّنى أو من الذى لا يضرّنى ؟ قالوا : من الذى يضرّك . قال : أفمِن
كلّ ضارّ لى أو من بعضهم ؟ قالوا : من كلّ ضارّ . قال : فإنّ
رسولُ البلاء أتانى ينعى إلىّ نفسى ومُلكى ، وزعم أنه يريد خراب ما عمرت

---

3 سكن: شكر A || 4 نكفك: نكفيك A || 9 السلاح: الصلاح AB LM
12 مطيفون: تطوفون B || 18 تحفظونى: تمنعونى AM BL || 21 ينعى: فنعى AM
BL (B فبقى) || 21 وزعم: ويزعم BL AM ||

you were my intimates and my helpers." They answered: "Oh King! where is this enemy, can he be seen or can he not be seen?" He said: "His trace can be seen but he himself cannot be seen." They said: "Oh King! This is our preparedness as you see it, and we can be relied upon and amongst us are clever and shrewd people. Show him to us that we do for you all that can be done." He answered: "I have been very much deceived in you and I have misplaced my trust when I chose you and took you as my protection. I have lavished riches upon you and I have raised your position and I have made you my entourage to the exclusion of others in order that you protect me from my enemies and guard me from them. Then I have undertaken to help you in that by strengthening the towns and fortifying the cities and giving you reliable weapons, and have kept away from you cares, and I have set you free in order to act as a guard for me. I did not anticipate to be alarmed while you were with me. I was not afraid of fate overcoming what I have built while you were attending on it; but now I have been overcome while you were round me and I have been attacked while you were with me. If that was weakness on your side I have not arranged my affairs safely and if it was negligence on your part you are no trustworthy advisers and are not my friends."

They answered him and said: "Oh King! With regard to danger which we can avert with cavalry and strength, we hope that will not reach you, if God wills, as long as we are alive; but the knowledge of that which cannot be seen is hidden from us and our strength is not great enough for it." He said: "Have I not chosen you to defend me from my enemies?" They answered: "Yes." He asked: "From which kind of enemy will you defend me? From the one who harms me or from the one who does not harm me?" They said: "From the one who harms you." He said: "From all who harm me or from some of them?" They said: "From everybody who harms you." He said: "The messenger of decay has come to me giving me news of my own death and that of my kingdom and has asserted that he wants the

وهدم ما بنيت ، وتفريق ما جمعت ، وفساد ما أصلحت ، وتبذير ما أحرزت ، وتبديل ما عملت ، وتوهين ما وثّقت ؛ وزعم أنّ معه الشماتة من الأعداء وقد قرّت .بى أعينهم ؛ فإنّه يريد أن يعطيهم منى شفاء صدورهم ؛ وذكر أنه سيهزم جيشى ، ويوحش أنسى ، ويُذهب عزّى ، ويؤتم ولدى، ويفرّق جموعى ، ويفجع .بى إخوانى وأهلى وقرابتى ، ويقطع أوصالى ، ويُسكن مساكنى أعدائى .

قالوا : أيّها الملك ! إنّما نمنعك من الناس والسباع والهوامّ ودوابّ الأرض ؛ فأمّا البلى فلا طاقة لنا به، ولا قوّة لنا عليه، ولا امتناع لنا منه . قال : فهل من حيلة فى دفع ذلك عنى ؟ قالوا: لا . قال : فشىء دون ذلك تطيقونه ؟ قالوا : ماهو؟ قال : الأوجاع والأحزان والهموم . قالوا : أيّها الملك ! قدر هذه الأشياء قوىّ لطيف ، وذلك يثور من الجسم والنفس ، وهو يصل إليك إذا لم توصل ، ولا يُحجب عنك ، وإن حجب لم يحتجب . قال : فأمر دون ذلك . قالوا : وماهو ؟ قال : ماقد سبق من القضاء. قالوا : أيّها الملك ! ومَن ذا غالبَ القضاء فلم يُغلب ، ومَن ذا كابره فلم يُقهر . قال : فماذا عندكم ؟ . قالوا : مانقدر على دفع القضاء؛ وقد أصبتَ التوفيق والتسديد . فماذا الذى تريد ؟ قال: أريد أصحابا يدوم عهدهم ، ويفوا لى ، وتبقى لى أخوّتهم ، ولا يحجبهم عنّى الموت ، ولا يمنعهم البلى عن صحبتى، ولا تستحيل بهم الأطماع عن نصيحتى،

---

[10] قال B فقال AM || [19] ويفوا AM ويوفوا BL || [20] نصيحتى L النصيحة B صحبتى AM

destruction of that which I have built up; the demolition of what I have constructed and the dispersal of what I have collected; the ruin of what I have well arranged and the dissipation of what I have achieved, and the changing of what I have done and the weakening of what I had firmly established, and he asserts that he brings along malicious joy from the enemies who are glad, seeing me in my distress, because he wants to give satisfaction to their spiteful hearts. He also mentioned that he will defeat my army and bereave me of my ease and will destroy my glory and make my children orphans and will disperse what I have collected and will distress my brethren and my relatives through my disaster, and he will sever my connections and give over my dwellings to my enemy."

They answered him: "Oh King, we can only defend you from men and wild animals and vermin and beasts of the earth, but over decay we have no power and no strength in us, and we are unable to give protection against it." Then he said: "Is there any device for defending me from that?" They said: "No." He said: "But can you help me in something else, lesser than death?" They said: "What do you mean?" He said: "Sorrow and grief and cares." They said: "Oh King! God who is powerful and benevolent has ordered these things, and this arises from the body and the soul. And this reaches you when you cannot be reached; no chamberlain can keep it away because it does not obey the chamberlain's orders." He said: "And something less than this?" They said: "And what is that?" The King said: "Preordained destiny." They said: "Oh King! Can anybody try to fight destiny without being defeated and can anyone strive against it without being overcome?" He said: "So what have you to say?" They said: "We are not able to ward off destiny. You have obtained success and prosperity; what is it that you want?" He said: "I want friends whose fidelity is permanent and who are faithful to me and whose friendship remains with me and whom death does not keep away from me and decay does not keep away from my company;

ولا يفردونى إن متّ ، ولا يُسلمونى إن عشت ، ويدفعون عنّى
ما عجزتم عنه من أمر الموت . قالوا : أيّها الملك ! ومَن هؤلاء
الذين وصفتَ ؟ قال : هم الذين أفسدتهم بإصلاحكم . قالوا :
أيّها الملك ! أفلا تصطنع عندنا وعندهم معروفا ؛ فإنّ
أخلاقك تامّة ، ورأفتك عظيمة . قال : إنّ فى صحبتكم السمّ
القاتل ، والصمم والعمى فى طاعتكم ، والبكم فى موافقتكم .
قالوا : كيف ذلك أيّها الملك ؟ قال : صارت صحبتكم إيّاى فى
الاستكثار ، وموافقتكم علىّ الجمع ، وطاعتكم إيّاى فى الاغتفال
فبطّأتمونى عن المعاد ، وزيّنتم لى الدنيا ؛ ولو نصحتمونى ذكّرتمونى
الموت ، ولو أشفقتم علىّ ذكّرتمونى البلى ، وجمعتم لى ما يبقى ،
ولم تستكثروا بما يفنى ؛ فإنّ تلك المنفعة التى ادّعيتموها
ضرر ، وتلك المودّة عداوة ؛ وقد رددتها عليكم ، لا حاجة لى
فيها منكم . قالوا : أيّها الملك الحكيم المحمود ! قد فهمنا
مقالتك ، وفى أنفسنا إجابتك ، وليس لنا أن نحتجّ عليك ؛
فقد رأينا مكان الحجّة ، فسكوتنا عن حجّتنا فساد لملكنا ،
وهلاك لدنيانا ، وشماتة لعدوّنا ، وقد نزل بنا أمر
عظيم بالذى تبدّل من رأيك ، وأجمع عليه أمرك . قال :
قولوا آمنين ، واذكروا ما بدا لكم غيرَ مرعوبين ؛ فإنّى
كنت إلى اليوم مغلوبا بالحميّة والأنفة ، وأنا اليوم غالب لهما ،
وكنت إلى اليوم مقهورا لهما ، وأنا اليوم قاهرهما ، وكنت إلى
اليوم ملكًا عليكم مملوكًا ، وأنا اليوم عتيق ، وأنتم اليوم من
مملكتى طلقاء . قالوا : أيّها الملك ! ما الذى كنتَ به مملوكًا إذ كنت علينا ملكًا ؟ قال : كنتُ

---

[2] ومن AM وما BL || [20] قاهرهما AL قاهر لهما BM || إلى اليوم AM بالأمس BL ||
[21] second اليوم om AM ||

also whom ambition does not turn away from giving me good advice and who do not desert me if I die and who do not give me up as long as I live, and ward off from me death—all that you are unable to do." They answered: "Oh King, and who are those whom you have described?" He answered: "They are those whom I have ruined by being good to you." So they said: "Oh King, cannot you grant your favour to us and to them, for your character is perfect and your kindliness is great?" He answered: "Verily in your friendship is deadly poison, in your obedience there is deafness and blindness and in your agreement is dumbness." They answered him: "How is this, oh King?" He said: "Your friendship for me is for gathering riches and your agreement with me is for amassing wealth and your obedience to me is in negligence. You have slowed me down from reaching the afterworld and you have embellished in my eyes this world. If you had wished to give me good advice you would have reminded me of death and if you had had pity on me you would have reminded me of decay and you would have collected for me what lasts and you would not have amassed what perishes. For this usefulness which you claim is harm, and this friendship is hostility; I hand them back to you, and do not want them from you."

They answered him: "Oh you wise and praiseworthy King, we have understood what you have said and we have in our mind an answer—though it is not up to us to argue with you. We see where the argument lies and to keep back these arguments in silence means the destruction of our kingdom and the end of our world—the malicious joy of our enemies. Your change of opinion and your decision is a heavy blow for us." He said: "Speak in safety and mention what occurs to you without fear, because I have up to now been overcome by passions and pride and now I am in control of both of them, and I have been until today defeated by them and now I am victorious over them, and up to now, though your king, I have been a slave but now I am free from that bondage and you are free from my kingship." They answered: "Oh you King, what had made

مملوكًا لهواى ، ومقهورًا بالجهل ، مستعبدًا لشهواتى ؛ فقد قطعت تلك الطاعةَ عنّى ، ونبذتها خلفَ ظهرى . قالوا : فقلْ ما أجمعتَ عليه أيّها الملك . قال : على القنوع والتخلّى لآخرتى وترك هذا الغرور ، ونبذ هذا الثقل عن ظهرى والاستعداد للموت ، والتأهّب للبلى ؛ فإنّ رسوله عندى قد ذكر أنه قد أُمِر بملازمتى ، والإقامةَ معى ، حتى يأتينى الموت . قالوا : أيّها الملك ! ومَن هذا الرسول الذى قد أتاك ولم تره ، وهو مقدّمةُ الموت الذى لانعرفه ؟ قال : أمّا الرسول فهذا البياض الذى يلوح بين السواد ، وقد صاح فى جميعه بالزوال فأجابوا له وأذعنوا . وأمّا مقدّمةُ الموت فالبلى الذى هذا البياض طرفه.

قالوا : أيّها الملك ! فلِمَ تدع مملكتك ، وتهمل رعيّتك ؟ وكيف لا تخاف الإثم فى تعطيل أمّتك ؟ ألسْتَ تعلم أنّ أعظم الأجر فى استصلاح الناس ، وأنّ رأس الصلاح الطاعةُ للأمّة والجماعة ؟ فكيف لاتخاف من الإثم وفى هلاك العامّةِ من الإثم فوق الذى ترجو من الأجر فى صلاح الخاصّةِ ؟ ألسْتَ تعلم أنّ أفضل العبادة العمل وأرشد العمل السياسةُ ؟ وأنّك - أيّها الملك - عدل على رعيّتك ، مستصلح لها بتدبيرك ، وأنّ لك من الأجر بقدر ما استصلحتَ ؟ أفلسْتَ - أيّها الملك - إذا خلّيتَ ما فى يديك من صلاح أمّتك فقد أردتَ فسادهم ؟ وإذا أردتَ فسادهم فقد حملتَ من الإثم فيهم أعظم ممّا أنت مصيب من الأجر فى خاصّةِ بدنك ؟ ألستَ - أيّها الملك - قد علمتَ أنّ العلماء قالوا : مَن أتلف نفسًا فقد استوجب لنفسه الفساد ، ومَن أصلحها فقد استوجب لبدنه الصلاح ؟ وأىّ فساد أعمّ من رفض

---

[1] ومقهورا AL مقهورا BM || [2] قطعت AM خالفت BL || [2] عن : خلف A || [7] قد om A || [9] يلوح : طرح A || [10] وأذعنوا له A || [11] فلم تدع AB أتدع L أفتدع || [14] وفى AB فى LM || [14] من الإثم om L || [16] وأرشد BL وان أشدّ AM || [17] استصلحت AM أصلحت BL || أفلست BL ألست AM

you a slave since you were our king?" He said: "I was enslaved by passions and dominated by ignorance, a slave to my desires; but I have now cut off this dependence from me and have thrown it behind my back." So they answered: "Say what have you resolved upon, oh King." He answered: "Upon moderation and to dedicate myself to my afterlife and to leave this deception and to throw this load from my back and to prepare myself for death and to get ready for decay, for its messenger is with me and has told me that he has been given the order to stick to me and stay with me until death comes." They said: "Oh King, who is this messenger, who came to you without our seeing him, this vanguard of death whom we do not know?" He answered: "The messenger is this white hair which has appeared in between the black: it announces the end of all of it, and they obey him and submit. The vanguard of death is decay, whose first sign is that white hair."

They said: "Oh King! Why do you leave your kingdom and neglect your subjects? How is it that the sin of leaving your people does not frighten you? Don't you know that the highest rewards are for those who do good to people and the highest good is the obedience to the community and to your people? And how are you not afraid of contracting a sin? Destroying the common people involves a sin which outweighs the merit which you hope to obtain by improving the elite. Don't you know that the best worship is good deeds and the most important deed is to occupy yourself with government of the people? And you, oh King, are just with your subjects, assuring their welfare by your government and you will get your reward according to the measure of the good which you have done. Is it not so, oh King, that when you neglect the welfare of your people which is entrusted to you, you wish for their ruin? And if you wished for their ruin, you have brought upon you more sin than the reward which you have achieved in looking only after yourself. Oh King, do you not know that the learned men say: 'who destroys a soul, himself deserves ruin, and who brings welfare to a soul deserves welfare for

هذه الرعيّة التى أنت إمامها ؟ و<أىّ صلاح أعمّ من> الإقامة فى
هذه الأمّة التى أنت نظامها ؟ حاشا لك أيّها الملك أن تخلع عنك
لباس المُلك الذى هو الوسيلة إلى شرف الدنيا والآخرة .

قال : قد فهمت الذى ذكرتم ، وعقلت الذى وصفتم . فإن كنتُ
إنّما أطلب المُلكَ عليكم للعدل فيكم ، والأجر من الله تعالى ذكره 5
فى استصلاحكم بغير أعوان يرفدوننى ، ووزراء يكفوننى ـ فما عسيت
أن أبلغ بالوحدة فيكم ؟ ألستم جميعا نُزَّعا إلى الدنيا وشهواتها ولذّاتها ؟
ولا آمَن أن أُخلِد إلى الدنيا التى أرجو أن أدَعها وأرفضها ؛ فإن فعلتُ
ذلك أتانى الموت على غرّة ؛ فأنزلنى عن سرير مُلكى إلى بطن
الأرض ، وكسانى الترابَ بعد الديباج والمنسوج بالذهب ونفيس الجوهر ، 10
وضمّنى إلى الضيق بعد السعة ، وألبسنى الهوان بعد الكرامة ؛ فأصير
فريدًا بنفسى ليس معى أحد منكم ؛ قد أخرجتمونى من العمران وأسلمتمونى
إلى الخراب ، وخلّيتم بين لحمى وسباع الطير وحشرات الأرض ؛ فأكلتْ
منّى النملة فما فوقها من الهوامّ ، وصار جسدى دودًا وجيفةً قذرة ؛
الذلّ لى حليف ، والعزّ منّى غريب . أشدّكم حبّا لى أسرعكم إلى دفنى ، 15
والتخلية بينى وبين ما قدّمت من عملى ، وأسلفت من ذنوبى ؛ فيورثنى
ذلك الحسرة ، ويعقبنى الندامة . وقد كنتم وعدتمونى أن تمنعونى من
عدوّى الضارّ ؛ فإذا أنتم لا منع عندكم ، ولا قوّة على ذلك لكم ولا سبيل .
أيّها الملأ ! إنى محتال لنفسى إذ جئتم بالخداع ، ونصبتم لى أشراك
الغرور . فقالوا : أيّها الملك المحمود ! لسنا الذى كنّا ، كما أنك 20
لست الذى كنت ، وقد أبدَلنا الذى أبدَلك ، وغيّرنا الذى غيّرك ؛

---

[12] منكم : فى الوحدة add BM || [13] وحشرات M وحشاش BL (الطير وحشرات om. A) || [18] منع : نفع A

himself', and what ruin is more far reaching than the abandonment of the community, whose leader you are, and what welfare is more far reaching than your staying in this nation whose ruler you are. Beware, oh King, that you throw off your princely garments which are the means to the glory of this world and of the afterworld!" He answered: "I have understood what you said and I have taken in what you have described to me. And if I had only sought a kingdom over you in order to do justice to you and in order to get a reward from God in justly establishing your affairs without helpers who would support me and vezirs who help me, what would I have reached alone among you? Are you not all wishing for this world and its desires and pleasures? And I cannot be sure that I would not turn to the world which I hope to leave and throw off. And if I were to do that, death would meet me unprepared and would make me descend from the throne of my kingdom to the depth of the earth and would clothe me in dust after brocade and tissue made of gold and precious stones, and it will confine me to narrowness after a wide space and will clothe me with contempt after an honorable position, and I shall be alone all by myself, none of you being with me. You made me come out from the inhabited world having handed me over to desolation and having given my flesh to wild birds and the insects of the earth and ants and other insects and my body will be vermin and an unclean corpse; humiliation is my companion and glory is a stranger to me. The one who pretends to love me most will be the quickest to bury me and to leave me alone with my former deeds, and the sins which I had committed before. This will bestow grief upon me and will bring about remorse as its consequence. You had promised me that you would defend me from my harmful enemies; behold you cannot defend me and there is no strength for that in you, and no way. Oh, you assembly, I shall find a way for myself since you have come with deceit and have put up the trap of deception." Then they answered him: "Oh you praiseworthy King, we are not what we were, just as you are not what you were. And what has changed

فلا تردّ علينا توبتنا، وبذل نصيحتنا. قال: أنا مقيم فيكم ما فعلتم ذلك،
ومُفارقكم إذا خالفتموه.

فأقام ذلك الملك فى مُلكه، وأخذ جنوده بسيرته واجتهدوا
فى العبادة؛ فخصبت بلادهم، وغلبوا عدوّهم، وازداد مُلكهم؛
حتى هلك ذلك الملك، وقد سار فيهم بهذه السيرة اثنتين وثلاثين 5
سنة؛ فكان جميع ما عاش أربعا وستين سنة.

II

قال بوذاسف: قد سُررت بهذا الحديث جدّا؛ فزِدْنى من
نحوه ازددْ سرورًا، ولربّى شكرًا. قال الحكيم:

زعموا أنه كان ملك من الملوك الصالحين، وكان له جنود
يخشون الله عزّ وجلّ ويعبدونه. وكان فى مُلك أبيه شدة 10
من زمانهم، والتفرّق فيما بينهم، وتنقّص العدوّ من بلادهم. وكان
يحثّهم على تقوى الله عزّ وجلّ وخشيته والاستعانة به، ومراقبته
والفزع إليه. فلمّا ملك ذلك الملك قهر عدوّه، واستجمعت رعيّته
وصلحت بلاده، وانتظم له الملك؛ فلمّا رأى ما فضّله الله عزّ وجلّ
به أترفه ذلك وأبطره وأطغاه؛ حتى ترك عبادة الله عزّ وجلّ وكفر 15
نعَمه، وأسرع فى قتل مَن عبَد الله. ودام مُلكه وطالت مدّته
حتى ذهل الناس عمّا كانوا عليه من الحقّ قبل ملكه ونسوه
وأطاعوه فيما أمرهم، وأسرعوا إلى الضلالة. فلم يزل على ذلك فنشأ فيه الأولاد،

---

2 خالفتموه AM خالفتمونى BL

9 وكان له جنود: الذين A || 10 عزّ وجلّ AL || 15 وأبطره AM فأبطره AL || 16 عبد الله LM عند عليه AB || مدّته: أيّامه A || 18 أمرهم AL أمرهم به BM

you has changed us too and what has made you different has made us different too. So do not reject our repentance and the advice we give you." So he answered: I shall abide with you as long as you act like this but I shall separate from you if you change your mind."

So this king stayed in his kingdom and his army took to his way of life and they were very eager in their devotion to God. The country was flourishing and they overcame their enemies and their realm increased until this king died after he had lived in that way for 32 years and the whole span of his life was 64 years.

THE STORY OF THE SKULL—IS IT A KING'S OR A PAUPER'S?

Būdāsf said: "I have enjoyed this story very much but now tell me something similar to it to increase my pleasure and my thanks to God." The wise man answered him and said:

People report that there was an upright king who had armies who feared God and worshipped Him. And there had been very difficult times during the reign of his father and quarrels between them and the enemy had taken away part of the country. But the son used to incite them to godliness and the fear of God Almighty, to ask Him for help and take heed of Him and take refuge in Him. And when that king had been made king he conquered his enemy and his subjects were united and the country prospered and the kingdom under him was well arranged. And when he saw all the excellent things which God Almighty had given to him, this led him to luxury and made him reckless and tyrannical so that he gave up worshipping God Almighty and he was ungrateful for His bounty and rushed into killing those who worshipped God. His kingdom lasted a long time until the people forgot and neglected righteousness which existed before he became king, and they quickly went astray and obeyed him in whatever he ordered them, and he did

وصار لا يُعبد الله عزّ وجلّ فيهم ، ولا يُذكر بينهم اسمه ولا يحسبون
أنّ لهم إلهًا غير الملك . وكان ابن الملك قد عاهد اللهَ عزّ وجلّ
فى حياة أبيه إنْ هو ملَك يومًا أن يعمل بطاعة الله عزّ وجلّ
بأمر لم يكن مَن قبله من الملوك يعملون به ولا يستطيعونه.
فلمّا ملَك أنساه المُلك رأيه الأوّل ، ونيّته التى كان عليها، وسكر
سُكر صاحب الخمر ، فلم يكن يصحو ويفيق .

وكان من أهل لطف الملك رجل صالح أفضل أصحابه منزلةً عنده،
فتوجّع له مما رآى من ضلالته فى دينه ، ونسيانه ما عاهد الله عليه.
وكان كلما أراد أن يعظه ذكر عتوّه وجبروته . ولم يكن بقى
من تلك الأمّة غيره ، وغير رجل آخر فى ناحية أرض الملك ؛
لا يُعرف مكانه ولا يُدعى باسمه . فدخل ذات يوم على الملك
بجمجمة قد لفّها فى ثيابه؛ فلمّا جلس عن يمين الملك انتزعها
من ثيابه فوضعها بين يديه ثم وطئها برجله ؛ فلم يزل يفركها بين
يدَى الملك وعلى بساطه حتى دنس مجلس الملك ممّا تحاتّ من
تلك الجمجمة . فلمّا رآى الملك ما صنع غضب من ذلك غضبًا
شديدًا ، وشخصت إليه أبصار جلسائه ، واستعدّت الحرس
بأسيافهم انتظارًا لأمره إيّاهم بقتله ، والملك فى ذلك مالك لغضبه.
وقد كانت الملوك فى ذلك الزمان على جبروتهم وكفرهم ذوى أناة
وتؤدة ؛ استصلاحًا للرعيّة ، وحرصًا على عمارة أرضهم ؛ ليكون ذلك
أعزّ للجانب وآدى للخراج . فلم يزل الملك ساكتًا على ذلك حتى
قام من عنده ؛ فلفّ تلك الجمجمة فى ثوبه . ثم فعل ذلك

---

[1] after يعبد A adds أحد || [3] بطاعة AM من طاعة BL || [4] بأمر AM بأمر من BL

not stop doing this. In this condition the children grew up and they did not worship God Almighty and amongst them His name was not mentioned and they did not reckon that they had a god apart from the king. But the son of the king had promised God Almighty during the lifetime of his father that if he became king one day, he would obey God Almighty in a thing which none of the previous kings had either done or been able to do. But when he became king, the kingship made him forget his first resolve and the aim which he had put before himself and he intoxicated himself as do those who are addicted to wine, and he did not wake up from his stupor.

"There was amongst the intimates of the king a pious man who amongst his friends held the highest position with the king. This man was grieved about the errors in his religious behaviour in which he saw him involved and about his forgetfulness of what he had vowed to God beforehand. And every time he wanted to give advice he remembered his insolence and tyranny. And no one was left of this community but he and another man in a distant part of the dominion of the king, of whom one did not even know where he stayed and whose name was not mentioned. Now one day he entered the king's palace with a skull which he had hidden under his garment and when he had sat down on the right of the king he took it out of his garment and put it before him, then he stamped on it with his foot and did not stop rubbing it before the king and on his carpet until the room was soiled from what broke off from this skull. When the king saw what he had done he became very angry and the looks of the attendants turned to him and the guards prepared their swords awaiting his order to them to kill him; but the king controlled his anger. The kings were at that time in spite of their tyranny and unbelief deliberate and patient, out of consideration for the welfare of their subjects and out of eagerness for the building up of their country, so that that should bring about an increase in their power and should help the collection of taxes. So the king continued to be silent until the man moved away from him,

فى اليوم الثانى والثالث .

فلمّا رآى أنّ الملك لا يسأله عن تلك الجمجمة ولا يستنطقه فى شىء من شأنها أدخل مع تلك الجمجمة ميزانًا وقليلاً من التراب ، فلمّا صنع بالجمجمة كما كان يصنع أخذ الميزان وجعل فى إحدى كفّتيه درهمًا ، وفى الأخرى بوزنه ترابًا ، ثم جعل ذلك التراب فى عين تلك الجمجمة ، ثم أخذ حفنة من التراب ووضعها فى موضع الفم من تلك الجمجمة. فلمّا رآى الملك ما صنع عيل صبره وبلغ مجهده ، فقال لذلك الرجل: قد علمت أنك إنّما اجترأت على ما صنعت لمكانك منّى ، وإدلالك علىّ ، وفضل منزلتك عندى ، ولعلّك تريد بما صنعت أمرا .

فخرّ الرجل للملك ساجدًا ، وقبّل قدميه ، وقال : أيّها الملك! أقبِلْ علىّ بعقلك كلّه ؛ فإنّ مثَل الكلمة كمثَل السهم ، إذا رُمِى به فى أرض ليّنة يثبت فيها ، وإذا رُمِى فى الصفا لم يثبت ، ومثَل الكلمة كمثَل المطر ، إذا أصاب أرضًا طيّبة مزروعة ينبت فيها، وإذا أصاب السباخ لم ينبت . وإن أهواء الناس متفرّقة ، والعقل والهوى يصطرعان فى القلب ؛ فإن غلب الهوى العقلَ عمل الرجل بالطيش والسفه، وإن كان الهوى هو المغلوب لم يوجد فى أمر ذلك الرجل سقطة. فإنى لم أزل مذ كنت غلامًا أحبّ العلم وأرغب فيه وأوثره على الأمور كلّها ، فلم أدع علمًا إلّا بلغت منه أفضل مبلغ . فبيْنا أنا ذات يومٍ أطوف بين القبور إذا بصرت بهذه الجمجمة بارزة من قبور المُلوك فغاظنى موقعها ، وفراقها جسدها غضبًا للمُلوك ؛ فضممتُها إلىّ ، وحملتها إلى منزلى فألبستها الديباج ونضحتها بالماء الورد ووضعتها على

---

[1] فى : عن B عنْ فى M || [3] وقليلا : وجفنات L || [4] صنع بالجمجمة : وضع الجمجمة A || كما : ما AL MB || [6] جفنة : قبضة M

[13] فيها : بها A || [19] منه : فيه A || [20] إذا : (وإذا أنا قد) A (إذ قد) M add قد || بهذه : بإناء الخمر M || [22] بالماء الورد : بالماء الورد والطيب AL هذه BL هذه AM B

wrapping up his skull in his garment, then he did that again on the second and third day.

When he saw that the king did not ask him about that skull and did not question him about anything connected with this matter he brought in together with his skull scales and a little dust, and after he had done to the skull what he had done before, he took the scales and put into one of the plates one dram and into the other dust corresponding to its weight. Then he put the dust into the eye of this skull. Then he took a handful of dust and put it into the place of the mouth in that skull. When the king saw what he had done he lost his patience and he could not bear it any longer and said to this man: "I know that you have only dared to do what you have done because of your position with me and because you are allowed to take liberties with me and because of your exceptionally high position with me. Perhaps you have some special intention with what you have done."

Then the man prostrated himself before the king and kissed his feet and said: "Oh King, listen to me with all your intelligence because the word is like an arrow; when it is thrown onto soft ground, it is fixed in it, and when it is thrown on hard ground it is not fixed in it: and the word is also like the rain, if it falls on good ground which has been sown it produces shoots, and if it falls on marshy ground, it does not produce shoots. For the desires of men are varied and desires and intelligence wrestle with one another in the heart, and if desires overcome the mind then the man acts with recklessness and stupidity, but if the desires are those which are overcome, then no lapse occurs in the affairs of such a man. I, since the days of my youth have not ceased loving wisdom and coveting it and preferring it to everything and I have not left any branch of knowledge until I had reached the highest level in it. Now while I was walking about one day between the tombstones, behold my eye fell on this skull which protruded from the grave of the kings and the fact that it was lying there and was separated from its body filled me with indignation on behalf of the kings,

الفرش ، فقلت : إنْ كانت من جماجم المُلوك فيؤثّر فيها
إكرامى إيّاها ، وترجع إلى جمالها وبهائها ، وإنْ كانت
من جماجم المساكين فإنّ الكرامة لا تزيدها شيئا ، ففعلت
ذلك بها أيّاما فلم أستنكر من هيئتها شيئا . فلمّا رأيت ذلك
دعوت عبدا هو أهون عبيدى عندى فأهانها فإذا هى على (5)
حالة واحدة عند الإهانة والإكرام . فلمّا رأيت ذلك أتيت
الحكماء فسألتهم عنها ، فلم أجد عندهم علما بها . ثم علمت
أنّ الملك منتهى العلم ومأوى الحلم ؛ فأتيتك خائفًا على نفسى،
فلم يكن لى أن أسألك عن شىء حتى تبدأنى به . فأحبّ أن تخبرنى
أيّها الملك : أجمجمةُ ملك هى أم جمجمةُ مسكين ؟ فإنه لمّا (10)
أعيانى أمرها تفكّرت فى عينها التى كانت لا يملؤها شىء حتى
لو قدرَتْ على ما دون السماء من شىء تطلّعت على أن تتناول
ما فوق السماء ؛ فذهبت أنظر ما الذى يسدّها ؛ فإذا وزن درهم
من تراب قد سدّها وملأها ، ونظرت إلى فيها الذى لم يكن
يملؤه شىء فملأتْه قبضةٌ من تراب . فإنْ أخبرتنى أيّها الملك (15)
أنها جمجمةُ مسكين احتججت عليك بأننى وجدتها وسط
قبور المُلوك . ثم اجمع جماجم ملوك وجماجم مساكين فإنْ
كان لجماجمكم عليها فضل فهو كما قلت . وإنْ أخبرتنى أنها
من جماجم الملوك أنبأتك أنّ ذلك الملك الذى كانت هذه جمجمته
قد كان من بهاء المُلك وجماله فى مثل ما أنت فيه اليوم . فحاشاك (20)
أيها الملك أن تصير إلى حال هذه الجمجمةِ ؛ فتوطأ بالأقدام وتخلط
بالتراب ، ويأكلك الدود ، وتصبح بعد الكثرة قليلا ، وبعد العزّة ذليلا ،
وتُسدّ بك حفرة طولها أدنى من أربعةِ أذرع ، ويورث ملكك ، وينقطع خبرك ،

---

9 فأحبّ BL وأحبّ AM || 14 يكن AM يمكن BL || 16 بانى : AM add قد || 18 كان :
A كانت || 18 أخبرتنى AM قلت L || انها AL بأنها M (om B) || 20 وجماله :
BM add وعزّته || 23 وتسدّ بك AL وتسعك BL || 23 خبرك AM ذكرك BL

and I took it up and carried it to my house and I clothed it in brocade and sprinkled it with rosewater and I put it on a carpet and I said: If it belongs to the skulls of the kings, then my honouring will make a difference and it will return to its former beauty and splendour, but if it belongs to the skulls of poor people, then my honouring it will not have the slightest impact. And I did that to it for some days and did not think any of its appearance changed. When I saw this I called a servant who was the most humble of all my servants and he treated it with contempt, but this skull remained in its condition whether I honoured it or despised it. And when I saw that, I went to the sages and consulted them about the skull but I did not find that they had any knowledge of it. Then I remembered that the King is the most knowledgeable person and full of forbearance. Thus I have come to you fearing for my life and I did not dare to approach you with any questions before you started me off and I want you to tell me, oh king, whether this is a skull of a king or the skull of a poor man. For when I could not make out the truth about it I thought of its eye which nothing would fill: if it had power over what is below the heaven, it would seek to obtain what is above the heaven. And I began to consider what would cover it and fill it and behold the weight of one dram of dust had covered it and filled it and I looked at its mouth which nothing had filled and a handful of dust filled it. Now, oh king, if you tell me that this is the skull of a poor man, I shall answer you that I have found it in the midst of the tombs of the kings. Then I shall collect the skulls of the kings and the skulls of poor people, and if there is for your skulls any superiority over it, it is as you say, and if you tell me that they belong to the skulls of kings I inform you that the king who owned this skull had the same royal splendour and beauty as you have now. Beware, oh king, you approach now the condition of this skull and you will be trampled upon with feet, and you will be mixed up with dust and the worms will eat you, you will be little after you have been much, and after glory, you will be humble. A hole will

وتفسد صنائعك ، ويُهان مَن أكرمت ، ويُكرَّم مَن أهنت ، ويستبشر أعداؤك ، ويذلّ أعوانك ، ويحول التراب دونك. فإن دعوناك لم تسمع ، وإن أكرمناك لم تقبل ، وإن أهنّاك لم تغضب ؛ فيصير بنوك يتامى ، ونساؤك أيامى ، وأهلك يوشك أن يستبدلْن أزواجًا غيرك .

فلمّا سمع الملك ذلك فزع قلبه ؛ فانسكبت عيناه يبكى ويُعْوِل ، ويدعو بالويل . فلمّا رآى الرجل ذلك علم أنّ قوله قد استمكن من الملك ، وقوله قد أنجع فيه ؛ زاده ذلك جرأة عليه وتكريرًا لمَا قال . فقال له الملك : جزاك الله عنّى خيرا ، وجزى مَن حوْلى من العظماء شرّا . لعَمْرى لقد علمتُ ما أردتَ بمقالتك هذه ، وقد أبصرت أمرى . فسمع الناس خبره ؛ فتوجّه أهل الفضل إليه ، وختم له بخير ، وبقى عليه إلى أن فارق الدنيا.

III

قال ابن الملك : زِدْنى من هذا المثل . قال الحكيم :

زعموا أن ملكًا كان فى أوّل الزمان ، وكان حريصًا أن يولد له ، وكان لا يدع شيئا مما يعالج به الناس أنفسهم إلاّ أتاه وصنعه . فلمّا طال ذلك عليه من أمره حملت امرأة له من نسائه ؛ فولدت غلاما . فلمّا نشأ وترعرع خطا ذات يوم بخطوة وقال: معاذكم تخفّون . ثم خطا أخرى فقال : تهرمون . ثم خطا الثالثة فقال: ثم تموتون . ثم عاد كهيئته يفعل ما يفعل الصبىّ . فدعا الملك العلماء والمنجّمين فقال : أخبرونى خبر ابنى هذا . فنظروا

---

[1] صنائعك: ضياعك A || [7] علم: AL وعلم BM || [11] أمرى: بأمرى A || [12] إليه BM خطوة A بخطوة [18] || BL وضعته AM نشأ [18] || BL نحوه AM

contain you whose length is less than four cubits, your kingdom will be inherited by others, and information about you will be cut off and what you have created will be spoiled, those whom you have honoured will be despised, and those whom you have despised will be honoured. Your enemies will rejoice and your helpers will be humbled and the dust will segregate you from the world. If we call you, you will not hear and if we honour you, you will not receive it, and if we humiliate you, you will not be angry and your sons will be orphans and your wives will be widows, and it will happen soon that your wives will choose other husbands apart from you."

Now when the king heard that, his heart became grieved and his eyes flowed over while he cried and raised his voice in lament. And when the man saw this he knew that his speech had made an impression upon the king and influenced him deeply; that increased his boldness to repeat what he had said. Then the king said to him: "May God reward you on my behalf and may he on my behalf requite with evil the great people of my realm. By my life I have understood what you wanted to say with this speech of yours and you have understood my case. The people heard the news and the men of merit turned to him; and life was good, he remained like that until he died.

THE PRINCE WHO FLEES HIS HOME AND THEN REFUSES TO MARRY A PRINCESS

Then the son of the king said: "Tell me another parable." The wise man answered (saying),

They say in older times there was a king very keen to have a son and he left no cure untried which people employ. After a long time one of his wives became pregnant and bore a son. When he began to grow up he took a step one day and he said: "Beware you will be light." Then he took another step and he said: "You will become old." Then he took a third step and said: "You will die."

فى شأنه وأمره فأعياهم أمره، فلم يكن عندهم فيه علم. فلمّا
رآى الملك أنه ليس عندهم فيه علم دفعه إلى المُرضعين
فأخذوا رضاعه، إلاّ أن منجّما قال: إنه سيكون إماما. وجعل
عليه حرّاسا لا يفارقونه. حتى إذا شبّ انسلّ يوما من عند
مرضعته والحرس، فأتى السوق فإذا هو بجنازة، فقال: 5
ماهذا؟ قالوا: إنسان مات. قال: ما أماته؟ قالوا: كبر وفنيت
أيّامه ودنا أجله فمات. قال: وكان صحيحًا حيّا يمشى ويأكل
ويشرب؟ قالوا: نعم. ثم مضى فإذا هو برجل شيخ كبير،
فقام ينظر إليه متعجّبا، فقال: ماهذا؟ قالوا: رجل شيخ كبير،
قد فنى شبابه وكبر. قال: وكان صحيحًا ثم شاب؟ قالوا: 10
نعم. ثم مضى فإذا هو برجل مريض مستلقيا على ظهره،
فقام ينظر إليه ويتعجّب منه؛ فسألهم: ماهذا؟ قالوا:
رجل مريض. قال: وكان هذا صحيحًا ثم مرض؟ قالوا: نعم.
قال: والله لئن كنتم صادقين فإن الناس لمجنونون. فافتُقد
الغلام عند ذلك فطُلب فإذا هو فى السوق، فأتوه فأخذوه 15
وذهبوا به فأدخلوه البيت، فلمّا دخل البيت استلقى على قفاه
ينظر إلى خشب سقف البيت ويقول: كيف كان هذا؟
قالوا: كانت شجرة نبتت ثم صارت خشبا ثم قُطع ثم بُنى
هذا البيت ثم جُعل هذا الخشب عليه.

فبينا هو فى كلامه إذ أرسل الملك إلى الموكّلين به: 20
انظروا هل يتكلّم أو يقول شيئا. قالوا: نعم، وقد وقع
فى كلامٍ ماظنّنه إلاوسواسا. فلمّا رآى الملك ذلك وسمع

---

[3] فأخذوا فأُخذن BM || [4] إليه: عليه A || [5] مرضعته مرضعيه BL AM ||
[9] رجل هذا رجل AM BL || [10] صحيحا AL صغيرا BM
[11] from مستلقيا to مريض om LA (homoio-teleuton); from مستلقيا to عندهم فيه AM B [14] لمجانين LM لمجنون لمجنونون B [15] قال : فسألهم BL [16] after قفاه L has وطلب فإذا هو || برجل مريض قال وكان صحيحا ثم مرض قالوا نعم قال والله || فى السوق فأتوه فأخذوه وذهبوا به فأدخلوه البيت فلما دخل البيت استلقى قفاه

Then he became his own self again and did as children do. The king called the scholars and the astrologers and said to them: "Inform me about this son of mine!" They looked into his case and affairs but it puzzled them and they had no knowledge of it. When the king saw that they had no knowledge of it, he sent the boy to the wet nurses and they started to nurse him, but one of the astrologers said: "He will be a religious leader." Then he chose for him guardians who were not supposed to leave him. At last one day, when he had grown up, he slipped away from his nurse and guardians and went to the market and behold there he met a funeral procession and said: "What is this?" They answered: "This is a man who died." Then he asked: "What has made him die?" They answered: "He became old and his days dwindled and his appointed time came near, so he died." The prince asked: "Was he hale, alive, and walked and ate and drank?" They answered: "Yes." Then he went out and behold, he met a very old man and he started looking at him in astonishment and he asked: "What is this?" They answered: "A very old man whose youth has vanished and he has become old." He asked: "Was he hale and young, then he became grey?" They answered: "Yes." Then he went on and behold, he met a sick man who was lying on his back. He stood and looked at him with great astonishment and asked them: "What is this?" They said: "A sick man." He said: "Was he hale and then became sick?" They answered: "Yes." He answered: "Verily, if you are telling the truth then people are mad. And the youth was missed at that time and they searched for him and lo, he was in the market, and they came for him and got hold of him and took him away and brought him home. When he entered his home he threw himself on his back and he looked at the wood of the roof of the house and said: "What was that one day?" They answered him: "It was a tree which grew, then it was wood, then it was cut to pieces, then this house was built, then this wood was laid upon it.

Now while he talked like that the king sent for his servants to whom he had entrusted him (and said) "Look,

جميع مالفظ به الغلام دعا العلماء فسألهم فلم يجد فيه
عندهم علما ، إلا الرجل الأوّل ؛ فأنكر قوله ؛ فقال بعضهم:
أيّها الملك ! لو زوّجته ذهب عنه الذى ترى ، وأقبل وعقل
وأبصر . فبعث الملك فى الأرض يطلب ويلتمس له امرأة
5 من أحسن الناس وأجملهم فزوّجوها منه . فلمّا أخذوا
فى وليمة عرسه أخذ اللاعبون يلعبون والزمّارون يزمُرون.
فلمّا سمع الغلام جبلتهم وأصواتهم قال : ماهذا ؟ قالوا :
هؤلاء لعّابون وزمّارون جُمعوا لعرسك ؛ فسكت الغلام. فلمّا
فرغوا من العرس وأمسوا دعا الملك امرأة ابنه فقال لها : إنه
10 لم يكن لى ولد غير هذا الغلام ؛ فإذا دخلت عليه فالطفى به،
واقربى منه ، وتحنّى إليه . فلمّا دخلت المرأة عليه أخذت تدنو
منه ، وتتقرّب إليه ، فقال الغلام : على رِسْلِك ؛ فإن الليل طويل،
بارك الله فيك ، واصبرى حتى نأكل ونشرب . فدعا بالطعام
فجعل يأكل ؛ فلمّا فرغ جعلت المرأة تشرب ؛ فلمّا أخذ الشراب منها نامت.
15 فقام الغلام فخرج من البيت ، وانسلّ من الحرس والبوّابين
حتى خرج ، وتردّد فى المدينة ؛ فلقيه غلام مثله من أهل المدينة
فاتّبعه . فألقى ابن الملك تلك الثياب التى كانت عليه ، ولبس بعض
ثياب الغلام ، وتنكّر جهده ، وخرجا جميعًا من المدينة فسارا
ليلتهما ؛ حتى إذا قرب الصبح خشيا الطلب فكمنا. فأُتِيَت
20 الجارية عند الصبح ؛ فوجدوها نائمة. فسألوها : أين
زوجك ؟ قالت : كان عندى الساعة. فطُلب الغلام

---

11 وتحنّى: وتجى LM وتحتى (or وتحتبى) A ونحى B ‖ 15 من: من بين A ‖ 17 فألقى: وألقى BM ‖ ابن الملك : BM add عنه ‖ 19 فكمنا : فأكمنا A AL

whether he is talking or saying something." They answered him: "Yes, he has started saying things which we consider to be nonsense." When the king learnt that and heard everything that the boy had said, he called the scholars and consulted them, but he found no knowledge of it among them except in the first man, but he disliked what he said. Then one of them said: "Oh King, if you marry him off he will get out of that state in which you see him and will become intelligent and reasonable and will get insight." Then the king sent people round the country to seek for him a woman. And they found for him one, a most beautiful creature and most attractive, and they married her to him. When they started on the wedding festivities the musicians and the pipers started to play. When the young man heard the noisy crowd and their voices he said: "What is this?" They answered him: "They are players and musicians who are assembled for the sake of your wedding." Then the young man fell silent. Now when the wedding-feast was over and it became night, the king called the wife of his son and said to her: "Look, I have no other son except this one, so if you go to him be friendly with him, come near him and endear yourself to him." When the woman entered his room she started to approach him and tried to become familiar with him. The young man said: "Slowly, for the night is long, God bless you, so be patient until we have eaten and drunk." Then he called for food and he started eating. And when he stopped the woman started drinking and when the drink began to influence her she fell asleep.

Then the youth got up, went out of the house and stole away from his guardians and the doorkeepers until he was outside and he walked round in the city. There he met another young man like him of the people of his town. He followed him and the prince threw to him those garments which were upon him and put some clothes of the young man on instead, and he disguised himself as much as he could. Then the two of them went out together from the city and travelled the whole night. When it was near morn they became afraid that they would be pursued and they hid. Then

فلم يُقدر عليه . فلمّا أمسى الغلام وصاحبه سارا ؛ ثم جعلا
يسيران الليل ، ويكمنان النهار حتى خرجا من سلطان
أبيه ، ووقعا فى سلطان ملك آخر .

ولذلك الملك الذى صارا إلى سلطانه ابنة قد جعل لها
5 ألّا يزوّجها أحدًا إلّا من هويته ورضيته ، وبنى لها غرفة
عالية فى السماء ، مشرفة على الطريق ؛ فهى فيها جالسة
تنظر إلى كلّ مَن أقبل وأدبر . فبيناهى كذلك إذ نظرت
إلى الغلام يطوف فى السوق وصاحبه معه فى خلقانه ،
فأرسلت إلى أبيها : إنى قد هويت رجلا ؛ فإن كنتَ مزوّجنى أحدًا
10 من الناس فزوّجنى منه . فأُتيت أمّ الجارية فقيل لها : إنّ
ابنتك قد هويت رجلا ، وهى تقول كذا وكذا . فأقبلت إليها
فرحة حتى نظرت إلى الغلام فأروها إيّاه . فنزلت أمّها
مسرعة حتى دخلت على الملك فقالت : إن ابنتك قد هويت
غلاما . فأقبل الملك ينظر إليه . ثم قال : أرونيه . فأروْه إيّاه
15 من بُعد . فأمر أن يلبس ثيابًا فاخرة ، ونزل فسأله واستنطقه
وقال له : مَن أنت ؟ ومِن أين أتيت ؟ قال الغلام : وما سؤالك
عنّى . أنا رجل من مساكين الناس . فقال : إنك لغريب ، وما
يشبه لونك ألوان أهل المدينة . فقال الغلام : ما أنا بغريب .
فعالجه الملك أن يصدقه قصته فأبى . فأمر الملك أُناسًا
20 يحرسوه وينظروا أين يأخذ ولا يعلم بهم . ثم رجع
الملك إلى أهله فقال : رأيت رجلاً كأنه ابن ملك ،

---

[3] فى سلطان ملك آخر AL فى ملك سلطان آخر BM || [6] فى السماء om L || [7] فبيناهى كذلك om AB, L on margin; M فبينما || [14] غلاما AM رجلا BM (B this passage om) || [15] بعد AM بعيد BL || [16] له om AM || [17] أنت AM انك L || [19] first الملك om BL

the guardians came to the girl when it was morning and they found her asleep. So they asked her, "Where is your husband?" and she answered: "He was with me just now." So they searched for the young man, but they were not able to trace him. When the evening came the youth and his companion travelled on, so all the time they travelled during the night and hid during the day until they left his father's realm and found themselves in the realm of another king.

Now this king at whose realm they had arrived had a daughter to whom he had promised not to give her in marriage to anybody except someone whom she desired and with whom she was pleased. He built for her a chamber very high up in the heaven overlooking the road. In this chamber she was always sitting looking at everybody who approached or went away; while she was doing so suddenly her look fell on the young man who walked about in the market-place, accompanied by his companion in his torn garment. So she sent a messenger to her father saying: "I have fallen in love with a man and if you want to marry me to anybody, marry me to him." Then they went to the mother of the girl and she was told: "Your daughter has fallen in love with a man and she says so and so." Then she went to her daughter full of joy in order to look at the young man and they showed him to her. Then the mother descended hurriedly and entered the apartment of the King and she said to him: "Behold, your daughter has fallen in love with a young man." So the King proceeded to look. Then he said: "Show him to me." And they showed him to him from the distance and he ordered that he should be given smart garments. Then he descended and asked him and questioned him. He said: "Who are you and from where do you come?" The youth answered: "Why do you ask me? I am a man who belongs to the poor class of people." So the King answered: "You are a stranger and your colour is not like the complexion of the people of this city." Then the youth retorted: "I am not a stranger!" And the King tried hard to make him say the truth. But he refused. So

وماله حاجة فيما تراودونه عليه . فبعث إليه فقيل له : إنّ
الملك يدعوك . فقال الغلام : وما أنا والملك يدعونى ومالى
إليه حاجة ، ومايدرى مَن أنا؟ فانطُلق به على كره منه ؛ حتى
دخل على الملك . فأمر بكرسىّ فوُضع له فجلس عليه ، ودعا
الملك امرأته وابنته فأجلسهما من وراء الحجاب خلفه .
فقال له الملك : دعوتك لخير . إنّ لى ابنة قد رغبت فيك ،
أريد أن أزوّجها منك ؛ فإن كنت مسكينا أغنيناك ورفعناك
وشرّفناك . قال الغلام : مالى فيما تدعونى إليه حاجة ؛
فإن شئت ضربت لك مثلاً أيّها الملك . قال : فافعل .

فقال الغلام : زعموا أنّ ملكًا من المُلوك كان له ابن
وكان لابنه أصدقاء صنعوا له طعاماً ودعوه إليه ؛ فخرج
معهم فأكلوا وشربوا حتى سكروا وناموا . فاستيقظ ابن
الملك فى وسط الليل فذكر أهله ؛ فخرج عائداً إلى منزله ،
ولم يوقظ أحداً منهم . فبينا هو فى مسيره إذ بلغ منه
الشراب ، وبصر بقبر على الطريق ؛ فظنّ أنه رحله ؛
فدخله فإذا هو بريح الموتى ؛ فحسب ذلك ـ لِمَاكان
به من السكر ـ أنها رياح طيّبة ، فإذا هو بعظام لايحسبها
إلاّ فرشه الممهّدة ، وإذا هو بجسدٍ قد مات حديثا ،
وقد أروح فحسبه أهله ، فقام إلى جانبه فاعتنقه وقبّله ،
وجعل يعبث به عامّة ليلته . فأفاق حين أفاق ، ونظر حين
نظر فإذا هو على جسد ميت ، وريح منتنة ، قد دنّس
ثيابه وجلده ، ونظر إلى القبر وما فيه من الموتى ؛
فخرج وبه من السوء مايختفى منه من الناس أن ينظروا إليه

---

14 منه AM فيه BL || 15 وبصر : ونظر A || 15 رحله AL دخله B مدخل بيته M
19 فقام إلى جانبه om ABL || 23 منه من L به من M من AB

the King ordered some people to watch him and see—without him noticing—where he would go. After that the King returned to his family and said: "I have seen a man who looks as if he was the son of a king but—he says—he has no need for what you suggest to him." After that he sent a messenger to him to tell him: "The King summons you." The young man answered: "What have I to do with the King that he calls me? And I am not in need of him and he does not know who I am." But he was taken along against his will and was brought to the King. Then the King ordered a chair to be brought and it was put there for him, and the young man sat down upon it. The King called his wife and his daughter and he made them sit down beyond the curtain behind him. Then the King said to him: "I have called you for a good purpose. I have a daughter, who has conceived love for you. I want to marry her to you, and if you are poor we shall make you rich and we shall give you a high and noble position." The youth answered him and said: "I am not interested in the thing that you offer me but if you wish I shall tell you a parable, oh King." The King said: "Please do so."

So the youth began: "They say that a certain king had a son and the son had friends who prepared for him a meal and invited him to it. He went out with them and they ate and drank until they were drunk and fell asleep. But the prince woke up in the middle of the night and remembered his family and went out in order to return to his house without waking any of the others. Now while he was on his way drink overcame him. He saw a grave on his way and he thought that it was his place. So he entered the grave, and behold, it was smelling of the dead and he thought because of his drunken condition that it was a good smell. And in the grave were dead bones which he reckoned was a bed prepared for him and lo, there was a dead body, recently died, and it had a bad smell and he thought it was his wife: He went there, embraced it and kissed it, and he idly played with it the whole night. Then he woke up when he woke up, and he looked when he looked, and behold, he was upon

متوجّهًا إلى باب المدينة؛ فوجده مفتوحًا فدخله، حتى أتى أهله،
فرآى أنه قد أُنْعِم عليه حين لم يلقه أحد. فألقى عنه ثيابه تلك
واغتسل ولبس ثيابا أخرى وتطيّب. عمّرك الله أيها الملك:
أتراه راجعًا إلى ماكان فيه وهو يستطيع؟ قال: لا. قال: فإنى أنا هو.
5 فالتفت الملك إلى امرأته وابنته وقال: قد أخبرتكما أنه
ليس له فيما تدعونه إليه رغبة. قالت أمّها: قد قصّرت فى
النعت لابنتى والوصف لها أيّها الملك، ولكنّى أتيته خارجة
إليه ومكلّمته. فقال الملك للغلام: إنّ امرأتى تريد أن
تكلّمك وتخرج إليك ولم تخرج إلى أحد قبلك. فقال الغلام:
10 لتخرج إن أحبّت. فخرجت وجلست وقالت للغلام: تعال إلى ما
قد ساق الله إليك من الرزق والخير فأزوّجك ابنتى؛ فإنك
لو قد رأيتها وماقسم الله عزّ وجلّ لها من الجمال والهيئة
لاغتبطت. فنظر الغلام إلى الملك فقال: أفلا أضرب لك مثلاً؟
قال: بلى. قال: إنّ سرّاقا تواعدوا أن يدخلوا خزانة الملك
15 ليسرقوا؛ فنقبوا حائط الخزانة فدخلوها فنظروا إلى متاعٍ
لم يروا مثله قطّ، فإذا هم بقلّة من ذهب مختومة بالذهب فقالوا:
لا نجد شيئًا أفضل من هذه القلّة، هى من ذهب، مختومة بالذهب
والذى فيها أفضل من الذى رأينا. فاحتملوها ومضوا بها حتى دخلوا
غيضة لا يأمن عليها بعضهم بعضا؛ ففتحوها فإذا فيها أفاعٍ
20 فوثبن فى وجوههم فقتلنهم أجمعين.
عمّرك الله أيّها الملك: أفترى أحدًا علم بما أصابهم

5 أخبرتكما: أخبرتكم ABM أخبركما L ||
om أتيته A أتيته ومكلمة. B om خارجة L أتيته خارجة إليه ومكلمته :7
(reads ومتكلمته) M || 12 عج om AB || 13 لك LM لها AB || 19 عليها بعضهم بعضا:
AB عليها بعضا بعضهم LM || 19 فيها: فى وسطها A LM

a dead body which smelled terribly and the corpse had soiled his garment and his skin and he looked at the grave and the dead persons which were in it and left. He was in such an evil state that it made him hide from the sight of men while he was walking towards the gate of the city. He found it open, so he entered it and eventually he came to his family and he was glad that nobody met him. Then he threw his garments from him and washed and put other garments on and perfumed himself. May you live long oh king! Do you think that this man would like to return of his own free will to the state in which he was?" The king said: "No." Then the young man said: "I am such a man." So the king turned to his wife and daughter, and said to them: "I have told you before that he has no desire for what you have proposed to him." Then the mother said: "You have failed in describing my daughter and talking about her, oh King, but I shall go to him and talk to him." So the king said to the young man: "My wife wants to talk to you and come out to you, though she has never gone out to anybody before." Then the young man answered and said: "Let her come out if she likes to." So she came out and sat down with him and said to the youth: "Come to the sustenance and good things which God has given to you, for I want to marry my daughter to you. For if you would only see her and what amount of beauty and comeliness God has apportioned to her you would be delighted." Then the youth looked at the king and said: "Shall I still tell you a parable?" The king said: "Yes"

He said: "Some thieves had arranged to enter the treasurehouse of the king in order to commit a theft, and they pierced the wall of the treasurehouse and entered it and they looked at objects the like of which they had never seen and behold, they found a chest sealed with gold. So they said to one another: 'We cannot find anything which is better than this chest which is made out of gold, sealed with gold and whose contents will be even more beautiful than what we see.' So they carried it and

وما لقوا من تلك القلّة يراجع النظر إليها ؟ قال : لا . قال :
فإنى أنا هو .

فقالت الجارية لأبيها : ائذن لى فأخرج إليه بنفسى
فأكلّمه ؛ فإنه لو قد نظر إلىّ وإلى جمالى وحسنى وهيئتى
5 وما قسم الله عزّ وجلّ لى من الجمال لم يتمالك أن يحبّ .
فقال الملك للغلام : إن ابنتى تريد أن تخرج إليك ولم تخرج
إلى أحد قطّ . قال : لتخرج إن أحبّت . فخرجت إليه وهى
أحسن الناس وجها فقالت للغلام : هل رأيتَ مثلى قطّ أو أتمّ
أو أجمل أو أكمل أو أحسن ؟ وقد هوَيْتك وأحببتك .
10 فنظر الغلام إلى الملك فقال : أفلا أضرب لها مثلاً ؟ قال : بلى .

قال الغلام : زعموا أيها الملك أن ملكًا كان له ابنان
فأسر أحدهما ملك آخر ؛ فحبسه فى بيت وأمر ألاّ يمرّ
عليه أحد إلاّ رماه بحجر ؛ فمكث بذلك حينا . ثم إن أخاه
قال لأبيه : ائذن لى فأنطلق إلى أخى فأفديه وأحتال له . قال :
15 فانطلِقْ وخُذْ معك ماشئت من مال ومتاع ودوابّ . فاحتمل
معه الزاد والراحلة ، وانطلق معه المغنّيات والنوائح . فلمّا
دنا من مدينة ذلك الملك أُخبِر الملك بقدومه ؛ فأمر الناس
بالخروج إليه فخرجوا إليه ، وأمر له بمنزل خارج من
المدينة ، فنزل الغلام فى ذلك المنزل . فلمّا جلس فيه
20 فنشر متاعه وأمر غلمانه أن يبيعوا الناس ويساهلوهم فى بيعهم
ويسامحوهم ؛ ففعلوا ذلك . فلمّا رآى الناسَ قد شُغلوا بالبيع
انسلّ ودخل المدينة وقد علم أين سجن أخيه . ثم أتى السجن فأخذ حصاة

---

[1] وما : after وفيها من الأفاعى M || adds B وفيها الأفاعى : القلة : علم
وما لقوا من تلك القلة يراجع النظر إليها بما أصابهم M لقوه يدخل يده فى تلك القلة
يجيب : يحب [5] om AB || من الجمال [5] BM || وأُكلّمه AL فأكلّمه [4] || A L?
الغلام وقالت للغلام وقدّا M adds : وجها [8] || رجل M أحد AL [7] || M; B?
له. om AB || [19] from فنزل to فيه om AB; وطرفا وهيكلا فسلّمت على || [14]
L has the words on the margin || [21] ويسامحوهم om AB

walked away with it until they entered some bushes, for none of them trusted the other. Then they opened it and behold, in it were snakes who jumped into their faces and killed all of them. God give long life to you, oh King. Do you think anybody who knew what happened to them and what they experienced with this chest would look at it again?" The king said: "No." He said: "I am like these."

Then the girl said to her father: "Give me permission to go out to him myself and talk to him, because if only he would look at me and at my beauty and comeliness and shape and the beauty which God has apportioned to me he could not help loving me." So the King said to the young man: "My daughter wants to come out to you though she has never done that for anybody." He answered: "Let her come out if she feels like it." So she came out to him and she had the most beautiful face in the world. Then she said to the young man: "Have you ever seen anything like me, more perfect and more beautiful, more accomplished and more comely? I have fallen in love with you and like you." Then the young man looked at the king and said: "Shall I tell her a parable?" The King answered: "Yes."

The young man said:"They relate, oh King, that a king had two sons and one of them was taken prisoner by another king who locked him up in a house and gave the order that nobody should pass him without throwing a stone at him, and he remained in that condition for a time. Then his brother said to his father: 'Give me permission that I may go to my brother, ransom him and use stratagems on his behalf.' The king said: 'Go, and take with you as much money and goods and as many mounts as you wish.' So he went, and took with him provisions, singing girls and wailers. When he approached the city of that king, the king got news of his approach and he ordered his people to go out to him which they did. He ordered a house for him outside the city. The youth took up his quarters in that house, and when he had settled down in it he spread out his

فرمى بها لينظر ما بقى من نفس أخيه . فصاح حين أصابته
الحصاة وقال : قتلتنى . ففزع الحرس عند ذلك وخرجوا
إليه وسألوه : لم صحت وما شأنك وما بدا لك ؟ ولا رأيناك
تكلّمت ونحن نعذّبك منذ حين وتُضرب ويرميك كلّ
من يمرّ بك بحجر ، ورماك هذا الرجل بحصاة فصحت
منها . فقال : إن الناس كانوا من أمرى على جهالة ورمانى
هذا على علم . فانصرف أخوه راجعًا إلى منزله ومتاعه ،
وقال للناس : إذا كان غدا فاتونى أنشر عليكم برّا ومتاعا
لم تروا مثله قطّ . فانصرفوا يومئذ حتى إذا كان من الغد
غدوا إليه بأجمعهم ؛ فأمر بالبرّ فنُشر ، وأمر بالمغنّيات
والنائحات وكلّ صنف معه مما يلهى به الناس ؛ فأخذوا فى
شأنهم فاشتغل الناس . فأتى أخاه فقطع عنه أغلاله ، وقال :
إنى مداويك . فاختلسه وأخرجه من المدينة ؛ فجعل على
جراحاته دواء كان معه ، حتى إذا وجد راحة أقامه على
الطريق ، ثم قال له : انطلق فإنك ستجد سفينة قد سُيّرت
لك فى البحر . فانطلق سائرا فوقع فى جبّ فيه تنّين ،
وعلى الجبّ شجرة نابتة ؛ فنظر إلى الشجرة فإذا على
رأسها اثنا عشر غولا ، وفى أسفلها اثنا عشر سيفا ،
وتلك السيوف مسلولة متعلقة . فلم يزل يتحمّل ويحتال
حتى أخذ بغصن من الشجرة وتعلّق به وتخلّص . وسار
حتى أتى البحر فوجد سفينة قد أُعدّت له إلى
جانب الساحل ؛ فركب فيها حتى أتوا به أهله .

---

[3] ولا AB وما LM || [4] وتضرب AB ويضربك M ونضرب قدميك ونضرب قدميك L . [8] عليكم : لكم A || [10] عليه om A || فأمر : فأمروا A || فنشره LM فنشروا AB || [15] سيّرت لك فى البحر AM نشرت لك فى البحر B نشرت لك فى البحر أعلامها L || [19] متعلّقة AB معلّقة LM || [20] وتعلق AL فتعلّق MB

wares and he ordered his servants that they should sell to the people and they should make a favourable price and be easy with them; and so they did. Then when he saw that the people were busy with buying, he stole away and entered the city, having found out where the prison of his brother was. Then he came to the prison and took a stone and threw it in order to find out whether his brother was alive. The brother cried out when the stone hit him and said: 'You have killed me!' His guard was alarmed about that and they went out to him and asked him: 'Why did you cry out? and what is the matter with you? What has happened to you for we have never noticed that you have said a word although we have tortured you for a long time and we have hit you and every one who passed you threw a stone at you. But when this man threw a stone at you, you cried out.' So he answered them and said: 'See, these people did not know anything about my affairs, but this man has thrown a stone at me knowingly.' And his brother turned round to go back to his house and to his wares. Then he talked to the people and said: 'Come to me again to-morrow, I shall spread out for you silk clothes and other wares, the like of which you have never seen.' So they went home that day but the next morning they returned all together and he ordered the clothes to be brought and they spread them out and he ordered the singers and mourners, and with it all the things by which people are amused, and they started with their business, and the people were occupied. Then he went to his brother and he cut his fetters off and said to him: 'I shall heal you.' And he got him out secretly and led him away out of the city, and he applied to his wound a medicine which he had on him and when he thought he had recovered he sent him on his way and said to him: 'Be off, for you will find a ship which has been prepared for you by the sea.' So the brother went away and fell into a hole in which was a dragon and above the hole was a tree firmly established and he looked at the tree and, behold, at the top of the tree were twelve demons and at its lower parts were twelve swords and these swords

عمّرك الله أيّها الملك : أتراه عائدا إلى ماقد عاين و لقى ؟ قال : لا .
قال : فإنى أنا هو .

فيئسوا منه . فجاء الغلام الذى صحبه من مدينته فسارّه
وقال : اذكرنى لها وأنكحنيها . فقال الغلام للملك : إن هذا
يقول إنْ أحبّ الملك أن ينكحنى ابنته فعل . فقال الملك :
لأفعل . ثم قال له : أفلا أضرب لك مثلا ؟ قال : بلى .

قال : إن رجلا كان فى قوم ، فركبوا سفينة فساروا فى
البحر ليالى . ثم انكسرت سفينتهم بقرب جزيرة فى البحر
فيها الغيلان ، فغرقوا كلّهم سواه ، فألقاه البحر إلى
الجزيرة ، وكانت الغيلان يشرفون من الجزيرة إلى
البحر . فأتى غولا فهوته ونكحها ، حتى إذا كان مع الصبح
قتلته وقسّمت أعضاءه بين صواحبها . واتفق مثل ذلك
لرجل آخر ، وأخذته ابنة ملك الغيلان فانطلقت به فبات
معها ينكحها . وقد علم الرجل مالقى مَن كان قبله فليس
ينام حذرا ، حتى إذا كان مع الصبح قامت الغول فانسلّ
الرجل حتى أتى الساحل ، فإذا هو بسفينة فنادى أهلها
فاستغاث بهم ، فحملوه حتى أتوا به أهله . فأصبحت
الغيلان فأتوا الغولة التى كانت معه فقالوا لها : أين
الرجل الذى بات معك ؟ قالت : إنه قد فرّ منّى .
فكذّبوها وقالوا : أكلتِه واستأثرتِ به
علينا . فلنقتلنّك إن لم تأتِنا به . فمرّت فى الماء حتى

---

3 من مدينته om LM

5 إنى أحبّ الملك أن ينكحنيها فعل (فقبل A) : إن أحبّ الملك أن ينكحنى ابنته فعل
فقال om AB فقال الملك لا أفعل || M إنى أحب أن ينكحنيها الملك AB
|| A om M ليالى وأيّاما BL ليالى 8 || BM قال L قال الغلام A قال له 6 || M لا أفعل
|| LM صواحباتها AB صواحبها 12 || M فهويها BL فهوتها : فهوته 11
AB كانت 18 || LM واستغاث AB فاستغاث 17 || LM فأخذته AB وأخذته 13
LM باتت

were unsheathed, hanging up. He tried to hold fast and find a way out, until finally he got hold of a branch of the tree and he hung on to it and he saved himself. So he went on until eventually he came to the sea and he found a ship which had been prepared for him by the side of the shore and he sailed in it until it brought him to his family. May God give you long life, oh King. Do you think that he would return to what he had seen with his own eyes and what he had met with?" The King said: "No." So the young man said: "I am in the position of that man."

So they despaired of him. So the young man who accompanied him from his city came forward and talked to him secretly and said: "Remember me to her, and give her in marriage to me." Then the youth said to the King: "Listen, this young man says, perhaps the king will kindly consent to marry his daughter to me." The King said: "I shall do so. He said: "Should I not tell you another parable?" He said: "Yes."

He said: "There was a man together with some company and they sailed on a boat on the sea for some nights. Then their ship broke near an island which was in the middle of the sea in which ghouls lived. Then all of them with the exception of himself drowned. Now the sea threw him onto the island and the ghouls looked on from the island towards the sea. He went to one ghoul and she fell in love with him and he married her, but when the morning dawned she killed him and divided his limbs between her friends. Then the same thing happened to another man. The daughter of the king of the ghouls got hold of him and she went away with him, and she spent the night with him and he made love to her. But the man knew what had happened to the one who was before him and he could not sleep because he felt so worried. When it was morning, the ghoul got up and the man stole away and went to the shore and lo and behold, he met a ship. He hailed the people on it and asked them for help and they took him along and eventually they had brought him to his family. And in the morning the ghouls woke up and came to the ghoul which

أتته فى منزله ورحله ؛ فدخلت وجلست عنده ، وقالت له: ما
لقيت فى سفرك هذا ؟ قال : لقيني بلاء خلّصنى الله منه.
وقصّ عليها ذلك؛فقالت : وقد تخلّصت ؟ قال : نعم. قال
فقالت : إنى أنا الغولة ، وجئت لآخذك . فقال لها:أنشدك
الله ألاّ تهلكينى ؛ فإنى أدلّك مكانى على رجل . قالت:إنى
أرحمك . فانطلقا حتى دخلا على الملك . قالت : اسمع منّا
أصلح الله الملك . إنى تزوّجت بهذا الرجل ، وهو من
أحبّ الناس إلىّ . ثم إنه كرهنى وكره صحبتى ؛ فانظر
فى أمرنا . فلمّا رآها الملك أعجبه جمالها ؛ فخلا بالرجل
وسارّه وقال له : إنى قد أحببت أن تتركها فأتزوّجها.
قال : نعم . أصلح الله الملك ما تصلح إلاّ له . فتزوّج بها
الملك ، وبات معها ؛ حتى إذا كان مع السحر ذبحته،
وقطعت أعضاءه ، وحملته إلى صويحباتها. أفترى
أيّها الملك أحداً يعلم بهذا ثم ينطلق إليه ؟ قال: لا.

قال الخاطب للغلام : لا أفارقك ، ولا حاجة لى فيما
أردتُ. فخرجا من عند الملك يعبدان الله جلّ جلاله،
ويسيحان فى الأرض . فهدى الله عزّ وجلّ بهما أناسا
كثيرا ، وبلغ شأن الغلام وارتفع ذكره فى الآفاق.فذكر
والده فقال : لو بعثت إليه لاستنقذته ممّا هو فيه؛فبعث
إليه رسولا فأتاه فقال له: ابنك يقرئك السلام.
وقصّ عليه خبره وأمره ؛ فأتاه والده وأهله،
فاستنقذهم مما كانوا فيه.

2: لقيني AB لقيت LM || 3 قال om LM || فإنى : إنى L om M || 4 الغولة AM
الغول BL || 17 ويسيحان: ويسبحان BL || عزّ وجلّ om AB || 20 له: إن L ان M

had been with him and said to her: 'Where is the man, who has spent the night with you?' She answered: 'He has escaped from me.' Then they accused her of lying and said: 'You have eaten him and you have kept him exclusively to yourself, neglecting us. But now we will kill you, if you do not bring him to us.' And she crossed the sea until she reached him in his abode and house. So she entered and sat with him and said to him: 'What has happened to you on this journey?' He answered: 'Misfortune has overtaken me but God has saved me from it, and he told her what had happened.' So she said: 'But now you are safe.' So he answered: 'Yes.' Then she said: 'I am that ghoul and I have come here to fetch you.' He said: 'I implore you in the name of God not to ruin me and I shall guide you instead of me to another man.' She answered: 'I have pity on you.' Then they went away until they entered into the presence of the king. She said: 'Listen to us, your majesty. I got married to this man whom I love better than anybody else, then he disliked my company. Now look into our case.' Now when the king saw her he was full of admiration for her beauty and he took the man aside and talked to him in secret, saying: 'I should like you to give her up so that I can marry her.' The man answered: 'Yes, your majesty, she does not befit anyone but the king.' And the king got married to her and spent the night with her until the morning came, when she slaughtered him and cut up his limbs and carried him to her companions. Do you think, oh king, that somebody who knows about this, would walk into it with open eyes?" He said: "No."

The prospective bridegroom said to the young man: "I do not want to separate from you and do no longer wish for what I wanted to do." Then they went out together from the palace of the king serving God, be His majesty exalted, and wandered through the lands. God led many people to the right way through them. The fame of the young man became great and his reputation was held high in many countries. Then he remembered his father, and said: "I should perhaps send someone to him in order to save him from the condition in which he is." So he sent a messenger to him, who came to him and said: "Your son bids you greetings;" and he told him his news and how he was. So his father and his family went to him and he saved them from the condition in which they were.